Fairy-Tech Academy

Z Thornton

Published by Z Thornton, 2024.

FAIRY-TECH ACADEMY

First edition. March 17, 2024.

ISBN: 979-8224224432

Written by Z Thornton.

Chapter 1: The Invitation

In a quaint town where the hum of machinery intertwined with the whispers of spells, Lila's home stood as the perfect blend between magic and machinery. The walls, adorned with ancient runes, were lit by softly glowing tech-lamps. Lila, with her sun-kissed hair and eyes that shimmered like a twilight horizon, was the embodiment of this duality. Her lineage, intellectual inventors and grand enchantresses, had bestowed upon her an innate curiosity for both realms.

As she sat in her room, her fingers danced between crafting a tiny gear and tracing a protective spell. The room itself was a mirror to her soul, half-filled with mechanical contraptions and half with enchanted artifacts.

As she meticulously adjusted a tiny gear on her latest invention, a soft fluttering sound caught her attention. A silver raven, its metallic feathers reflecting the sunlight, perched on her windowsill, holding a shimmering envelope in its beak.

Lila approached with a mix of caution and curiosity. The raven, seemingly understanding her intent, gently placed the envelope on the sill before taking off, leaving behind a trail of sparkling dust. The envelope itself was a marvel. Crafted from a material that felt like the softest parchment, it gleamed with an iridescent sheen. Embedded within were tiny circuits that pulsed with a soft light, creating intricate patterns reminiscent of ancient magical symbols.

With bated breath, Lila carefully opened the envelope. Inside was a card made of the same gleaming material. As she touched it, the symbols began to move, rearranging themselves to form words. "Dear Lila," it began, "You are cordially invited to join the Fairy-Tech Academy." The words were accompanied by an emblem – a gear intertwined with a wand, symbolizing the perfect blend of technology and magic.

The prestige of the academy was known to all in the town. It was where the brightest minds delved into the mysteries of magic and the wonders of technology. To receive an invitation was an honor few could dream of, and it spoke volumes about the recipient's potential.

Lila's heart raced with excitement and anticipation. The academy was a place where her dual passions could flourish, where the debates of her parents would find harmony. Holding the invitation close to her heart, she imagined the adventures that awaited her, the challenges she'd face, and the legacy she was destined to create.

The news of the invitation spread through Lila's home like wildfire. By evening, the entire family had gathered in the living room, the shimmering envelope placed ceremoniously on the coffee table. The room was filled with a palpable mix of excitement, apprehension, and curiosity.

Lila's mother, a renowned technologist in the town, was the first to speak. "The Fairy-Tech Academy," she mused, her fingers tracing the emblem on the envelope. "It's an honor, Lila. But remember, technology is the future. Magic, while fascinating, has its limitations."

Her father, a mage with a lineage that traced back to the town's founders, raised an eyebrow. "Magic is our heritage," he countered gently. "It's the essence of who we are. The academy recognizes the potential of merging both worlds. Lila has the best of both of us in her."

Caught between her parents' differing views, Lila looked to her younger sibling, Leo, for support. But Leo's face was clouded with envy. "Why her?" he muttered, barely audible, his fingers twitching as if itching to conjure a spell. "I've practiced magic twice as hard. It's not fair."

Before Lila could respond, her grandmother, the eldest in the room and a repository of the family's history, intervened. "Enough," she said, her voice carrying a weight that silenced the room. "This isn't about magic versus technology or who's more deserving. This is Lila's moment."

She turned to Lila, her eyes softening. "Child, this academy is a place of great learning, but it's also a place of great responsibility. The world is at a crossroads, and you have a chance to shape its path. Embrace both magic and technology, for together, they can achieve wonders."

The room was silent for a moment, each member lost in thought. Lila's grandmother, Neoma, beckoned her to sit beside her. The old fireplace crackled, casting dancing shadows on the walls of their modest home. Neoma's eyes, though aged, sparkled with the wisdom of countless years and countless tales.

"Before this town was a beacon of unity between magic and machinery," Neoma began, her voice soft yet commanding, "the world was divided."

Centuries ago, the land was split into two dominant factions: the Mages of Eldoria and the Technologists of Cyronis. Eldoria was a realm of enchantment, where the air shimmered with spells and the rivers flowed with potions. The Mages believed in the power of the natural elements, drawing strength from the earth, wind, fire, and water.

In contrast, Cyronis was a marvel of innovation. Towering skyscrapers, flying vehicles, and advanced machinery painted its skyline. The Technologists trusted in the might of metal and machine, harnessing energy from sources the Mages deemed unnatural.

For years, the two factions coexisted, separated by vast mountains and dense forests. But as both realms expanded, seeking more land and resources, their borders clashed, leading to the Great War. It was a battle not just of swords and shields, but of ideologies. The Mages, with their elemental spells, against the Technologists, with their mechanized armies.

The war raged for decades, tearing the land apart. Villages were decimated, forests burned, and rivers ran red. But amidst the chaos, a prophecy emerged. It spoke of a 'Chosen One', born of both magic and machine, who would bring an end to the conflict and unite the world.

The war reached its climax on the Night of the Crimson Eclipse. As the moon bathed the world in a deep red hue, the leaders of both factions met on the battlefield. But instead of clashing, they paused, realizing the futility of their feud. The prophecy had begun to weave its magic.

From the union of these leaders, a new realm was born, a town where magic and technology coexisted, complementing each other. The Mages shared their knowledge of the elements, while the Technologists introduced innovations that enhanced magical practices. The town became a symbol of harmony, drawing people from all corners of the world.

"But," Neoma's voice grew somber, "with unity came envy. A faction, born from the remnants of the war, lurked in the shadows. They believed in the purity of their respective ideologies and saw this union as an abomination. They are the Antagonists, and their goal is to tear apart what we've built. They have ensured that their factions exists up to this day."

Lila listened, rapt. She felt the weight of her lineage, the legacy of the 'Chosen One'. Neoma leaned closer, her voice barely above a whisper, "The academy's invitation isn't just an opportunity, Lila. It's a calling. The Antagonists are growing stronger, and the prophecy speaks of another 'Chosen One' who will face them. Our history isn't just in the past; it's unfolding now."

Neoma leaned back, her tale complete. The room was silent, save for the crackling of the fire. Lila's heart raced. The history of her world, the unity of magic and machine, and the lurking shadow of the Antagonists – it was a lot to take in.

But as she looked into her grandmother's eyes, Lila felt a surge of determination. She was ready to embrace her destiny, to protect the legacy of unity, and to face whatever challenges lay ahead.

Chapter 2: First Impressions and the Academy's Ambiance

The Fairy-Tech Academy stood tall and majestic, a testament to the harmonious blend of magic and technology. Its spires reached for the heavens, shimmering in the morning light, while the base was rooted deep into the ground, drawing strength from the earth's core. The walls, made of enchanted stone, sparkled with embedded circuits that pulsed with energy.

Lila stood at the academy's grand entrance, her heart pounding with a mix of excitement and trepidation. The massive gates, forged from a blend of enchanted metal and crystal, slowly opened, revealing the world inside. As she stepped in, the air around her seemed to vibrate, resonating with the power of both magic and machinery.

To her left, a fountain crafted of silver and sapphire bubbled with water that glowed in shifting hues, powered by a hidden tech mechanism. To her right, a tree with metallic leaves whispered secrets of ancient spells to those who dared to listen. The pathways were lined with luminescent stones, guiding students with their soft glow.

Students bustled around, some levitating books with spells, while others used tech gadgets to record notes. Lila could see classrooms where holograms merged with magical illusions, creating a unique learning experience. The harmony of the two worlds was evident everywhere, from the enchanted elevators to the tech-powered broomsticks.

Yet, amidst this marvel, Lila felt like a small fish in a vast ocean. The enormity of the academy, with its endless corridors and countless rooms, was overwhelming. She clutched the shimmering envelope, her invitation, as if it were a lifeline.

Suddenly, a soft chime echoed through the air, and a floating orb appeared before her. It was a blend of crystal and tech, pulsating with a gentle light. "Welcome to Fairy-Tech Academy, Lila," it greeted in a melodious voice. "I am Lumina, your guide. Shall we begin the tour?"

Lila nodded, her apprehension easing slightly. Lumina led her through the academy, showcasing the seamless integration of the two worlds. They passed by the Spell-Tech Labs, where students experimented with merging spells and circuits. The library, a vast expanse of books and digital archives, buzzed with activity. In the distance, Lila could see the training grounds where students practiced their skills, be it casting spells or operating advanced machinery.

As they moved, Lumina shared snippets of the academy's history and its vision. "The founders believed in a world where magic and technology could coexist, enhancing each other. And this academy is a manifestation of that dream," Lumina explained.

Lila's tour ended at the dormitories, a magnificent structure with towers that seemed to touch the sky. Each room was equipped with both magical amenities and tech gadgets, ensuring the comfort of its occupants.

Lila's room was on the fifth floor, overlooking the academy's gardens. As she stepped in, the room adjusted itself to her preferences, the walls changing color and the temperature setting itself just right. A welcome note, written in glowing letters, floated in the air, "Welcome home, Lila."

She sank into the plush bed, her mind racing. The academy was everything she had imagined and more. The blend of magic and tech, the possibilities it offered, was exhilarating. But she also knew that challenges lay ahead. The antagonistic faction's presence was palpable, and she had to be prepared.

Lila had barely settled into her room when a soft knock echoed through the space. She opened the door to find a girl with raven-black hair cascading down her back, her eyes a deep shade of violet. Intricate tattoos, reminiscent of ancient spells, adorned her arms, glowing faintly.

"Hi! I'm Elara," she introduced herself with a warm smile, extending a hand adorned with tech-infused rings. "I'm your roommate."

Lila's eyes widened in surprise. "Oh! I wasn't expecting anyone so soon. It's lovely to meet you, Elara."

Elara stepped inside, her gaze sweeping over the room. "I've been here for a while. Thought I'd give you some time to settle in before introducing myself."

Lila chuckled, "Thanks for that. This place is... overwhelming."

Elara nodded in agreement. "It can be. But you'll get used to it. The blend of magic and tech here is unlike anywhere else."

As the two chatted, Lila learned more about Elara's lineage. Her family had been integral in pioneering the integration of magic and technology. "My ancestors believed that the two worlds could enhance each other," Elara explained, her fingers tracing the glowing tattoos on her arm. "These tattoos? They're not just for show. They're a blend of ancient spells and modern tech, allowing me to channel energy more efficiently."

Lila's eyes sparkled with curiosity. "That's fascinating! My family has always been divided on the matter. My mother loves technology, while my father is all about Magic."

Elara laughed, "Sounds like lively dinner conversations at your place."

The two bonded over shared experiences, discussing the challenges and joys of growing up in a world where magic and tech coexisted. As they spoke, Lila noticed a peculiar device on Elara's wrist. It looked like a bracelet but pulsed with energy.

Noticing her gaze, Elara held it up. "This? It's a Magi-Tech Bracelet. It helps me balance the energy flow between my spells and tech gadgets. Want to try?"

Lila hesitated for a moment before nodding. Elara placed the bracelet on Lila's wrist, and instantly, a rush of energy coursed through her. She could feel the magic in her veins syncing with the tech in the bracelet, creating a harmonious rhythm.

"It's... incredible," Lila whispered, her eyes wide with wonder.

Elara grinned, "It's the beauty of merging two worlds. The possibilities are endless."

The two continued to chat, delving deeper into their backgrounds and aspirations. Lila learned that Elara aspired to further the integration of magic and tech, hoping to create devices that could benefit both mages and tech enthusiasts. In turn, Lila shared her dreams of exploring the unknown, of pushing the boundaries of what was possible.

As the evening wore on, the two realized they had more in common than they initially thought. Both were driven by a desire to make a difference, to leave a mark on the world.

Elara, sensing Lila's apprehension about the academy, offered words of comfort. "It can be daunting, I know. But remember, you're not alone. We're in this together."

Lila smiled, feeling a weight lift off her shoulders. "Thank you, Elara. I'm glad we met."

Elara winked, "So am I. Now, how about we explore the academy together tomorrow? There's so much to see!"

Lila nodded eagerly, "I'd love that."

As the two settled into their beds, the room bathed in the soft glow of their combined magic and tech, a bond was forged. A bond that would see them through the challenges and adventures that lay ahead.

***

The sun was high in the sky, casting a golden hue over Fairy-Tech Academy's sprawling grounds. Lila, with her newfound friend Elara, wandered through the maze-like pathways, absorbing the sights and sounds of her new environment. Their path led them to a secluded courtyard, where an unusual scene unfolded.

A tall young man with jet-black hair, wearing a leather jacket adorned with circuitry patterns, was deeply engrossed in a device that buzzed and whirred. Beside him, a petite girl with fiery red hair, dressed in a flowing robe, was chanting incantations, her hands moving in intricate patterns, creating a dance of shimmering lights around the device.

Lila's curiosity got the better of her. "Hi, I'm Lila," she introduced herself, "What's happening here?"

The young man looked up, his hazel eyes reflecting a sharp intelligence. "I'm Finn," he said with a nod of acknowledgment. "This is an Etheric Resonator. I'm trying to synchronize its tech components with magical energies."

The redhead, with a playful glint in her green eyes, added, "And I'm Maya. I'm here to ensure he doesn't blow up the academy with his experiments." She winked, causing Finn to roll his eyes.

Elara chuckled, "Always the drama queen, aren't you, Maya?"

Maya responded with a mock curtsy, "One must keep things interesting."

Lila laughed, sensing the camaraderie. "So, Finn, you're into tech?"

Finn leaned against a nearby tree, "Born and raised amidst wires and codes. My family pioneered many of the tech advancements in the city. But I've always been intrigued by the potential synergy between tech and magic."

Maya interjected, "While I hail from a lineage of powerful mages. Our ancestors were elemental masters, controlling fire, water, wind, and earth. But this academy, with its blend of magic and tech, felt like the right place to expand my horizons."

As the day progressed, Lila learned more about her new acquaintances. Finn spoke of his childhood, surrounded by gadgets and gizmos. He shared tales of his first invention at the age of ten, a wristwatch that could predict weather changes based on atmospheric magical energies. His passion for integrating tech with magic was palpable, and Lila could see the spark in his eyes as he spoke of his projects.

Maya's stories were of a different kind. She spoke of her family's vast library, filled with ancient tomes and scrolls. She described her early days, practicing spells under the watchful eyes of her elders, and the joy of mastering her first elemental spell. Her tales were filled with wonder, of moonlit rituals and magical creatures.

The courtyard soon became a hub of activity. Students gathered, drawn by Finn's device and Maya's display of magic. A synergy of tech and magic was a rare sight, even in Fairy-Tech Academy. Lila watched in awe as Finn and Maya effortlessly blended their skills, creating a spectacle that left the onlookers spellbound.

As the shadows lengthened, signaling the approach of evening, the crowd began to disperse. Lila, Elara, Finn, and Maya sat on the grass, their conversation flowing effortlessly. They spoke of their dreams and aspirations, their fears and challenges. It was evident that despite their diverse backgrounds, they shared a common bond, a mutual respect for each other's skills.

Finn, pulling out a small gadget from his pocket, said, "This is just the beginning. Imagine the possibilities when we truly merge the worlds of magic and tech."

Maya, plucking a leaf from a nearby plant and transforming it into a butterfly with a wave of her hand, added, "The future is limitless. And we're at the forefront of this revolution."

Lila, inspired by their passion, felt a renewed sense of purpose. She realized that Fairy-Tech Academy was not just an institution; it was a melting pot of ideas, a place where magic and tech coexisted, pushing the boundaries of what was possible.

As the quartet made their way back to the academy's main building, Lila felt a deep sense of gratitude. She had found friends who shared her passion, who understood her dreams. With Finn's tech genius, Maya's magical prowess, and Elara's guidance, Lila knew that her journey at Fairy-Tech Academy was going to be an unforgettable adventure.

***

The Fairy-Tech Academy was more than just a place of learning; it was a living testament to the harmonious blend of ancient magic and cutting-edge technology. As Lila wandered through its corridors, every corner seemed to hum with energy, every shadow whispered tales of old, and every beam of light showcased the marvels of innovation.

The walls of the academy bore intricate murals, each telling a story. On one side, legendary mages conjured storms and tamed beasts, while on the other, pioneers of technology harnessed the power of steam and electricity. These murals met in the middle, where mages and inventors worked together, their combined efforts leading to the creation of the academy itself.

Lila's footsteps echoed softly on the polished marble floors, leading her to the grand atrium. Here, a colossal tree stood, its roots intertwined with circuits and its branches adorned with glowing orbs. Students sat beneath it, some engrossed in holographic books, others practicing spells, and a few tinkering with gadgets. The tree, Lila realized, symbolized the academy's ethos: a fusion of nature and machine, magic and tech.

The sound of animated discussions drew Lila to a corner where a group of students debated fervently. Their topic was evident: the integration of magic with artificial intelligence. "Magic is about intuition and connection. Can a machine truly understand that?" argued one student. Another retorted, "But with technology, we can amplify our powers. Why limit ourselves?" It was clear that the academy encouraged such debates, creating an environment of intellectual curiosity.

Venturing further, Lila discovered the academy's vast library. Ancient tomes, their pages filled with spells and histories, stood alongside modern terminals where students accessed digital archives. In this space, the wisdom of the ages met the discoveries of the present, offering a comprehensive reservoir of knowledge.

A soft, melodious tune lured Lila to the music chamber. Here, students played instruments that were a blend of the old and new. Harps with electronic strings, flutes enhanced with auto-tuning, and drums that resonated with both magical and acoustic beats. The resulting symphony was otherworldly, a sound that transcended traditional boundaries.

As Lila continued her exploration, she came across the dining hall. The room buzzed with activity as students enjoyed meals that combined magical herbs with modern culinary techniques. A sip of a drink could invigorate one's magical energies, while a bite of a pastry might boost cognitive functions. The academy ensured that even meals became an experience of the blend of magic and tech.

But it was the observatory that truly took Lila's breath away. Perched at the academy's highest point, it offered a panoramic view of the surroundings. Here, students gazed at the stars, their patterns deciphered using both magical divination and advanced algorithms. The night sky, illuminated by constellations and the neon hues of the city, painted a picture of a world where the past and future coexisted.

As the day turned to evening, Lila found herself in the academy's garden. Luminescent flowers, a result of magical and genetic engineering, glowed softly, lighting up the paths. Mechanical birds flitted about, their songs harmonizing with the chirps of real ones. In the distance, a group of students practiced elemental magic, their spells interfacing with drones that responded to their commands.

Lila's exploration was interrupted by the chime of a bell, signaling the start of a special assembly. Students from all corners of the academy converged in the main hall. At the center stood a holographic stage where debates were held. Today's topic was the role of the antagonistic faction in the academy's history. As arguments were presented and countered, Lila realized that the academy was not just a place of learning. It was a microcosm of their world, reflecting its challenges, opportunities, and the ever-present dance between magic and technology.

Feeling a sense of awe and inspiration, Lila knew that the Fairy-Tech Academy was where she was meant to be. It was a place where dreams took flight, where the impossible became possible, and where the past and future melded to create a present full of endless possibilities.

Chapter 3: The Glimmering Goggles

The soft glow of the evening sun filtered through the curtains of Lila's dorm room, casting a warm hue over her desk. Scattered across the wooden surface were various sketches, diagrams, and notes. Lila's fingers danced over a piece of parchment, her quill moving with precision as she sketched an intricate design.

She paused, her eyes narrowing in concentration. The idea had been brewing in her mind for days, ever since she'd witnessed the seamless integration of magic and tech at the academy. What if there was a way to *see* the flows of both magic and technology? A device that could help one visualize the intertwining energies?

Lila's hand moved with renewed vigor as she began sketching a pair of goggles. These wouldn't be ordinary goggles. They would be embedded with tiny tech circuits and infused with magical runes. The lenses would be designed to capture and display the flows of both magic and tech, allowing the wearer to see the harmonious dance of energies.

She imagined herself wearing the goggles, walking through the academy, and witnessing the hidden patterns of magic and tech that lay beneath the surface. The corridors would come alive with swirling energies, and devices would reveal their magical cores. It would be a bridge between the two worlds, a tool to foster understanding and collaboration.

As she added the finishing touches to her design, Lila felt a surge of excitement. This could be revolutionary! She imagined students and professors using the goggles to enhance their learning and research, breaking down barriers between magic and tech enthusiasts.

But as with all great ideas, this one came with its challenges. The integration of magic and tech was no simple feat. It required a deep understanding of both domains and a delicate balance to ensure that the energies didn't clash. Lila knew she couldn't do it alone. She needed expertise, guidance, and most importantly, a partner who shared her vision.

She thought of Elara, her best friend, and a brilliant mage. Together, they could bring this idea to life. With a determined glint in her eyes, Lila rolled up her sketches and headed to the academy's library. It was time to dive deep into research and turn her vision into reality.

***

The vast expanse of the academy's library was a sight to behold. Towering bookshelves, filled with ancient tomes and modern manuscripts, stretched as far as the eye could see. The soft hum of floating candles and the occasional whisper of students engrossed in their studies added to the library's enchanting ambiance.

Lila, clutching her sketches tightly, scanned the room for Elara. She found her friend seated at a secluded table, surrounded by a pile of books. Elara's deep blue eyes, always filled with curiosity, widened in surprise as Lila approached.

"Lila! What brings you here?" Elara asked, her voice filled with genuine interest.

With a mixture of excitement and nervousness, Lila unfurled her sketches, revealing the design of the goggles. "I have an idea, Elara. A device that could let us see the flows of both magic and tech. But I need your help."

Elara leaned in, her gaze moving over the intricate design. "This... this is brilliant, Lila! But it's also ambitious. Merging magic and tech in such a manner... it's uncharted territory."

Lila nodded, her determination evident. "I know. That's why I came to you. Together, we can make this a reality."

Elara smiled, her enthusiasm matching Lila's. "Alright, let's start with some research. We need to understand the history, the past attempts, and the challenges faced in merging magic and tech."

The duo delved deep into the library's vast collection. Hours turned into days as they pored over ancient texts, scrolls, and manuscripts. They discovered tales of pioneers who had once tried to bridge the gap between magic and tech, only to face insurmountable challenges. Some had succeeded, while others had faced catastrophic failures.

One particular text caught their attention. It was an old leather-bound journal, its pages yellowed with age. The journal belonged to a mage named Galen, who had lived during the time of the great war. Galen had been obsessed with the idea of merging magic and tech and had documented his experiments in detail.

As Elara read aloud, Lila listened intently. Galen had created a device similar to Lila's goggles. However, his creation had been unstable, leading to unpredictable results. The journal hinted at a mysterious legacy, a powerful artifact that Galen believed held the key to a harmonious merger.

"The Ethereal Prism," Elara whispered, her voice filled with awe. "Galen believed that this artifact could balance the energies of magic and tech. But he never found it."

Lila's eyes sparkled with determination. "Then we'll find it, Elara. With the Ethereal Prism and our combined knowledge, we can make the goggles a reality."

Elara nodded, her resolve firm. "But we must tread carefully, Lila. Galen's journal speaks of dangers, of energies clashing and causing destruction. We need to understand these risks before we proceed."

The duo continued their research, uncovering more references to past experiments. They learned of mages and tech enthusiasts who had faced challenges similar to theirs. Some had achieved breakthroughs, while others had been consumed by their ambitions.

As the days turned into weeks, Lila and Elara became inseparable. They spent countless hours in the library, discussing theories, experimenting with designs, and seeking guidance from ancient texts.

Their bond grew stronger, forged by a shared vision and a determination to succeed.

One evening, as they sat amidst a pile of books, Elara looked up, her expression thoughtful. "Lila, we're on the brink of something extraordinary. But we must remember the lessons of the past. We must respect both magic and tech, understanding their strengths and limitations."

Lila nodded, her gaze filled with gratitude. "I couldn't have come this far without you, Elara. Together, we'll create a device that bridges the gap between magic and tech, helping with understanding and collaboration."

Elara smiled, her confidence unwavering. "And we'll do it with caution, ensuring that our creation brings harmony, not chaos."

As the duo continued their research, they were filled with a sense of purpose. They knew that the path ahead was filled with challenges, but they were determined to overcome them. With Elara's assistance and their combined knowledge, Lila's vision was one step closer to becoming a reality.

Challenges and Malfunctions

The sun streamed through the windows of Lila's dorm room, casting a golden hue over the scattered blueprints and tools. The room, once neat and orderly, now resembled a workshop, with components of both magical and technological origin strewn about.

Lila, her brow furrowed in concentration, carefully adjusted a tiny crystal within the frame of the goggles. Beside her, Elara was engrossed in a thick tome, her fingers tracing ancient runes as she murmured incantations.

"Alright," Lila announced, holding up the goggles with a triumphant smile. "Let's give this another try."

Elara nodded, setting aside the book. "Remember, slow and steady. We need to ensure the energies are balanced."

Lila slipped the goggles over her eyes, taking a deep breath. As she activated the device, a rush of images flooded her vision—swirling patterns of magical auras intertwined with the sharp, precise lines of technological circuits. For a moment, everything seemed perfect.

But then, without warning, the goggles flickered. A sharp jolt of energy coursed through Lila, causing her to cry out and rip the goggles off. The room was filled with the acrid smell of burnt circuits.

"Lila!" Elara exclaimed, rushing to her side. "Are you alright?"

Lila nodded, rubbing her temples. "I'm fine, just a bit dazed. The goggles... they malfunctioned."

Elara examined the goggles, her expression grave. "The energies clashed. We need to recalibrate and ensure the magic and tech components are in harmony."

The duo worked tirelessly, making adjustments and running tests. But each attempt was met with a new challenge. Sometimes the goggles would overheat, while other times they would simply go dark, refusing to function.

Frustration mounted as the days passed. Lila, ever the optimist, tried to keep their spirits up, but even she couldn't hide the disappointment in her eyes. Elara, on the other hand, grew more determined with each setback.

"We're missing something," Elara mused one evening, poring over the blueprints. "There's a key element we haven't considered."

Lila sighed, leaning back in her chair. "We've tried everything, Elara. Maybe it's just not possible to merge magic and tech in this way."

Elara shook her head. "No, I refuse to believe that. We've come so far. We just need to approach this from a different angle."

The breakthrough came unexpectedly. While experimenting with a new alloy for the goggles' frame, Elara stumbled upon a unique property. The alloy, when infused with a specific magical herb, acted as a buffer, preventing the energies from clashing.

With renewed hope, Lila and Elara integrated the alloy into the goggles' design. The results were promising. The goggles functioned smoothly, providing a clear view of both magical and technological flows.

However, the challenges didn't end there. As they continued their tests, they discovered that prolonged use of the goggles led to fatigue and dizziness. The merging of two distinct forces took a toll on the user's mind, making it difficult to discern reality from illusion.

"We need to add a safety mechanism," Lila declared. "Something that will automatically shut off the goggles if the user is at risk."

Elara nodded in agreement. "And we need to include a manual override as well. We can't afford any more unexpected malfunctions."

The duo worked diligently, refining the design and addressing the malfunctions. With each iteration, the goggles became more stable and reliable. But the journey was far from easy. They faced countless setbacks, each one testing their resolve and determination.

Yet, through it all, their bond grew stronger. They leaned on each other for support, drawing strength from their shared vision and unwavering belief in their mission.

As the days turned into weeks, Lila and Elara grew closer to their goal. The goggles, once a mere concept, were now a reality. But the challenges they faced served as a stark reminder of the complexities of merging magic and tech.

With the goggles finally functional, the duo looked ahead, eager to explore the possibilities and unlock the mysteries of their world. But they were also acutely aware of the risks and the weight of their responsibility.

For Lila and Elara, the journey had only just begun.

Whispers of Opposition

The grandeur of the academy's library was a sight to behold. Towering bookshelves, filled with ancient tomes and modern manuscripts, stretched as far as the eye could see. The soft glow of enchanted lanterns illuminated the vast space, casting a warm, golden hue over the polished wooden tables and plush reading chairs.

Lila and Elara, having made significant progress with the goggles, decided to delve deeper into their research. They hoped to uncover more about the mysterious legacy of merging magic and tech. With a list of references in hand, they scoured the library, pulling out relevant texts and cross-referencing information.

As the hours passed, the library began to fill with students. The soft murmur of whispered conversations and the rustling of pages created a soothing ambiance. Lila, engrossed in a book on ancient magical artifacts, barely noticed the passage of time. Elara, on the other hand, was meticulously transcribing notes from a particularly old and fragile manuscript.

It was then that they heard it—a hushed conversation from a nearby alcove. The voices were low, but the tone was unmistakably serious.

"...merging magic and tech is a fool's errand," a voice sneered. "Those two girls are playing with fire. They have no idea of the dangers they're inviting."

Another voice chimed in, "I've heard rumors about their project. Goggles that can see both flows? It's unnatural. The Council won't stand for it."

Lila and Elara exchanged a glance, realizing that they were the topic of discussion. They discreetly moved closer, trying to catch more of the conversation without being noticed.

A third voice, one that sounded familiar to Lila, added, "It's not just the Council. There are others, powerful factions within the academy, who believe that magic and tech should remain separate. They won't take kindly to such experiments."

The first voice laughed, "Those girls are in way over their heads. They think they're making groundbreaking discoveries, but they're just digging their own graves."

Elara's eyes narrowed, anger flashing in her gaze. She was about to confront the gossipers when Lila gently tugged at her arm, signaling for her to remain calm.

But it was the next voice that truly caught their attention. "You're all missing the point," it said, heavy with emotion. "This isn't just about some goggles or a misguided experiment. It's about legacy, about the weight of our ancestors' choices. And trust me, I know all about that weight."

Lila and Elara recognized the voice instantly—it was Cedric. The usually confident and composed young man sounded strained, revealing a vulnerability they had never witnessed before.

"The pressure to uphold family traditions, to meet expectations... it's suffocating," Cedric continued. "But we must remember our duty to the academy and to the world. Magic and tech have always been separate for a reason. Those who tried to merge them in the past faced dire consequences."

There was a pause, and then another voice, softer and more sympathetic, replied, "Cedric, we understand the burden you carry. But those girls, Lila and Elara, they're just curious students. They don't deserve to be dragged into this."

Cedric sighed, "I know. But they've already attracted attention, and not all of it is friendly. They need to be careful."

The conversation shifted, and the group began discussing other matters. Lila and Elara retreated to a more secluded section of the library, their minds racing.

"They know about our project," Elara whispered, her face pale. "And it sounds like there's more at stake than we realized."

Lila nodded, her expression thoughtful. "Cedric... I had no idea he felt that way. The weight of his family's legacy... it must be overwhelming."

Elara sighed, "We need to be cautious. If there are factions within the academy that oppose our work, we could be in real danger."

Lila looked determined. "We won't be intimidated. Our research is important, and we have every right to pursue it. But we'll be smart about it. We'll take precautions and ensure our work remains confidential."

Elara nodded in agreement. "We've come too far to back down now. But we also need to understand the history, the reasons behind the opposition. There's clearly more to this story than we know."

The duo resumed their research with renewed vigor, determined to uncover the truth behind the mysterious legacy of merging magic and tech. But the whispers of opposition served as a stark reminder of the challenges they faced.

As they delved deeper into the academy's secrets, Lila and Elara realized that their quest for knowledge was not just about innovation and discovery. It was also about understanding the past, navigating the complexities of tradition and progress, and finding their place in a world on the brink of change.

And as the shadows lengthened and the library's lanterns dimmed, the two young women knew that their journey was only just beginning.

Chapter 4: Unveiling the Unknown and the Mechanics of Magic-Tech

The sun streamed through the stained-glass windows of the Fairy-Tech Academy, casting a kaleidoscope of colors across the stone floor. Lila and Elara stood in the center of a spacious room, a small crowd of curious students gathered around them. The anticipation in the air was palpable.

Lila held the goggles in her hands, their intricate design shimmering in the sunlight. She took a deep breath, her heart racing. "Ready?" she asked Elara.

Elara nodded, her eyes filled with excitement. "Let's see what they can do."

Lila carefully placed the goggles over her eyes and adjusted the straps. For a moment, everything was dark. Then, as she activated the device, the world around her transformed.

The room was filled with swirling patterns of light and energy, intertwining and dancing around each other. The flows of magic and tech, previously invisible to the naked eye, were now laid bare for Lila to see. She gasped in wonder, taking in the breathtaking sight.

Elara, watching Lila's reaction, whispered, "What do you see?"

Lila turned to look at Elara, and her eyes widened in amazement. Elara was surrounded by a radiant aura, a blend of tech circuits and magical runes, seamlessly merging and flowing around her. "It's... it's incredible," Lila breathed. "I can see the magic and tech flows in everything. And they're... they're harmonizing."

The students who had gathered around them murmured in awe, eager to witness the goggles' capabilities for themselves. One by one, Lila allowed them to try on the goggles, each student reacting with astonishment and wonder.

"It's like seeing the world in a whole new light," one student exclaimed.

Another added, "I never realized how interconnected magic and tech truly are."

As the goggles were passed around, the room was filled with gasps of surprise and exclamations of delight. The students were captivated by the hidden patterns revealed by the goggles, and word quickly spread throughout the academy about Lila and Elara's groundbreaking invention.

However, amidst the excitement, there were also whispers of skepticism and concern. Some students questioned the ethics of merging magic and tech, while others worried about the potential dangers of the device.

But for Lila and Elara, the goggles represented hope and possibility. They had taken their first step towards bridging the gap between two worlds, and the potential of their invention was limitless.

As the sun began to set, casting a golden glow over the academy, Lila and Elara stood side by side, gazing out at the horizon. The journey ahead was uncertain, but they were ready to face whatever challenges lay ahead, united in their vision and determination.

Finn's Tech Insight

The excitement from the goggles' demonstration still lingered in the air as the students gathered in the academy's grand hall. A large stage had been set up, adorned with intricate machinery and glowing runes. At the center of it all stood Finn, his eyes sparkling with enthusiasm.

"Ladies and gentlemen," he began, his voice resonating through the hall, "today, I have the privilege of showing you something truly extraordinary. A fusion of magic and technology that has the potential to change our world."

The crowd leaned forward, captivated by Finn's words. Lila and Elara exchanged excited glances, knowing that Finn's demonstration would be a perfect complement to their own work.

Finn gestured to a sleek device on the table beside him. "This," he said, "is the Arcanum Engine. A marvel of engineering that harnesses the raw power of magic and channels it through technological circuits."

He activated the device, and the room was filled with a soft hum. The Arcanum Engine came to life, its core glowing with a mystical light. The students watched in awe as Finn manipulated the controls, causing the engine to emit a series of harmonious tones.

"What you are witnessing," Finn explained, "is the result of years of research and experimentation. The Arcanum Engine is able to detect and interpret magical frequencies, translating them into mechanical energy. It's a symphony of science and sorcery."

He paused, letting the significance of his words sink in. "But that's not all. The true beauty of this invention lies in its ability to adapt and evolve. By integrating magical runes with adaptive algorithms, the Arcanum Engine can learn and grow, becoming more efficient and powerful over time."

Finn's passion for his work was evident in every word he spoke. He moved around the stage with grace and confidence, demonstrating the various functions of the Arcanum Engine. He showed how it could be used to power machinery, enhance spells, and even heal wounds.

As he spoke, he wove a narrative that transcended mere technical details. He painted a picture of a world where magic and technology were not separate entities but intertwined like threads in an exquisite garment. A world where innovation and imagination could break down barriers and open new horizons.

Lila and Elara listened intently, their minds racing with possibilities. Finn's demonstration was more than just a showcase of his expertise; it was a vision of the future. A future they were all striving to create.

The demonstration concluded with a flourish, as Finn activated a series of interconnected devices, all powered by the Arcanum Engine. The machinery whirred to life, performing a complex dance of precision and elegance. The crowd erupted into applause, their faces alight with wonder and inspiration.

Finn bowed, a satisfied smile on his face. "Thank you," he said, his voice filled with genuine gratitude. "Together, we can forge a new path. A path that embraces the best of both worlds and leads us to a brighter tomorrow."

As the students filed out of the grand hall, their minds buzzing with ideas and excitement, Lila and Elara approached Finn. They congratulated him on his success and expressed their admiration for his work.

Finn's eyes twinkled as he looked at them. "You two are on the brink of something incredible," he said, his voice soft and sincere. "Your goggles are a testament to what can be achieved when we dare to dream and push the boundaries of what's possible."

He placed a hand on Lila's shoulder and looked into her eyes. "Never lose sight of your vision," he said. "The world needs dreamers like you."

With those words, he left them, his footsteps echoing down the hall. Lila and Elara stood in silence, their hearts filled with determination and hope.

They knew that they were part of something much larger than themselves. A movement that was gaining momentum, fueled by innovation, courage, and a shared belief in the potential of magic and technology.

Finn's demonstration had provided insight into the principles behind magic-tech integration and ignited a spark within them. A spark that would guide them on their journey and inspire them to reach for the stars.

Maya's Contribution

The Fairy-Tech Academy's grand hall was abuzz with excitement. After the groundbreaking demonstrations by Lila, Elara, and Finn, the students eagerly awaited the next presentation. The spotlight shifted to Maya, a young mage with a lineage that traced back to some of the most powerful sorcerers in history.

Maya stepped onto the stage, her posture confident, her eyes gleaming with determination. She was known for her unparalleled knowledge of ancient magical patterns, and today, she was about to showcase a device that was the culmination of her research.

"Good afternoon," she began, her voice clear and resonant. "Today, I present to you the Aether Compass, a device that deciphers the intricate patterns of magic and technology, guiding us to the perfect fusion of both."

She held up a delicate, ornate device that shimmered with an ethereal glow. The Aether Compass was a marvel to behold, with intricate runes etched onto its surface and a pulsating core that seemed to dance with both magical and technological energy.

Maya activated the device, and the hall was bathed in a soft, radiant light. Patterns began to emerge on the walls, floors, and ceilings—patterns that seemed to be a blend of ancient magical symbols and modern technological circuits.

"These patterns," Maya explained, "represent the harmonious convergence of magic and technology. The Aether Compass deciphers these patterns, allowing us to tap into the limitless potential of their fusion."

The students watched in awe as Maya demonstrated the device's capabilities. She directed the Aether Compass towards various objects in the room—a centuries-old spellbook, a state-of-the-art computer, a magical potion, and a technological gadget. Each time, the device revealed patterns that were previously hidden to the naked eye.

Lila and Elara exchanged impressed glances. They could see the immense potential of Maya's invention and how it could complement their own work with the goggles.

As Maya continued her demonstration, the reactions of her peers were a mix of admiration, intrigue, and a hint of envy. Whispers filled the hall, with many students marveling at the significance of Maya's mage lineage and her innate ability to bridge the gap between the ancient and the modern.

However, it wasn't just the device that captivated the audience. Maya's eloquence, her deep understanding of both magic and technology, and her passion for integration shone through every word she spoke. She wasn't just presenting a device; she was sharing a vision—a vision of a world where magic and technology coexisted in perfect harmony.

As her demonstration drew to a close, Maya addressed the audience with a heartfelt plea. "The future lies in our hands," she said, her voice filled with emotion. "We have the tools, the knowledge, and the passion to create a world where magic and technology are not at odds but are partners in progress. Let us embrace this vision and work together to make it a reality."

The hall erupted into applause, with many students giving Maya a standing ovation. Lila and Elara approached her, their faces beaming with admiration.

"That was incredible, Maya," Lila said, her voice filled with genuine appreciation.

Elara nodded in agreement. "Your Aether Compass is a game-changer. Together, we can achieve so much more."

Maya smiled, her eyes glistening with tears of joy. "Thank you," she whispered. "Together, we will change the world."

Cedric's Observation

The grand hall of the Fairy-Tech Academy buzzed with the vibrant energy of innovation and discovery. Students and professors congregated, eager to witness the unveiling of groundbreaking magic-tech integrations. Amidst the crowd, a figure stood resolute in his convictions, yet couldn't help but be drawn into the spectacle before him: Cedric.

Cloaked in robes adorned with the emblem of his family—a lineage staunchly dedicated to the preservation of pure magic—Cedric observed from a shadowed corner. His piercing blue eyes scrutinized every demonstration, every flicker of light, and every technological marvel presented.

As the hall erupted into applause following Maya's presentation, Cedric's hands remained firmly at his sides, his expression stern yet thoughtful. The innovations were indeed impressive, a testament to the ingenuity of the young minds at the academy. But to Cedric, they were nothing compared to the raw and untamed power of pure magic, a force that had been revered by his family for generations.

His grandfather's words echoed in his mind, a constant reminder of the path he was destined to follow. "Magic is the essence of our being, Cedric. It is a force that should remain untainted by the mechanizations of technology."

Despite the wonders unfolding before him, Cedric couldn't shake the feeling that this fusion was a desecration of the sacred art his family had cherished for centuries. The technological marvels, though fascinating, were but pale imitations of the grandeur and majesty that magic held in its purest form.

His contemplation was interrupted by the hushed voices of his peers, members of the faction that upheld the purity of magic. Their words resonated with Cedric, reaffirming his belief in the sanctity of their cause.

"Blasphemy," one muttered with disdain, a sentiment that Cedric found himself agreeing with, despite the flicker of curiosity that had momentarily ignited within him.

Alaric, his cousin and a fellow advocate for magic purity, beckoned him over. "Cedric, we must stand united against this sacrilege. Our heritage, our very identity is at stake."

Cedric nodded, his resolve hardening. The allure of technology, he realized, was a dangerous siren's song, tempting him to stray from the path of righteousness. But he would not falter. His loyalty to his family and their beliefs outweighed the fleeting wonder he had experienced.

As Alaric voiced his concerns, Cedric stood tall, a beacon of unwavering conviction amidst a sea of innovation and change. "We cannot allow our sacred traditions to be overshadowed by this... this abomination," Cedric declared, his voice ringing with authority.

The two shared a moment of understanding, their shared beliefs binding them together. As the demonstrations continued, Cedric's determination grew. He would show the academy the true might of magic, undiluted and unmatched. The world of technology had its wonders, but to Cedric, they would always remain a distant second to the ancient and powerful art of magic.

Chapter 5: Secrets of the Underground

The Fairy-Tech Academy was a sprawling structure, its spires reaching for the skies and its foundations buried deep within the earth. Lila, with her insatiable curiosity, often found herself wandering its labyrinthine corridors, seeking out its secrets. Today was no different.

She had been tracing the flow of a peculiar magical current, one that seemed to pulse with both the rhythm of tech and the fluidity of magic. It led her to a forgotten part of the academy, where the walls were thick with age and the air heavy with the scent of old books and rusted metal.

As she ventured deeper, her fingers brushed against a wall, revealing a hidden latch. With a soft click, a concealed door swung open, revealing a dimly lit chamber. Lila's heart raced as she stepped inside, her mage-light illuminating the vast expanse.

The chamber was a treasure trove of history. Tables were strewn with blueprints, sketches, and half-finished devices. There were shelves lined with dusty tomes, their pages filled with notes on merging magic and tech. In the center stood a grand workbench, its surface scarred from countless experiments.

Lila approached the workbench, her fingers tracing the etchings of ancient runes and circuitry. She picked up a tarnished device, its design reminiscent of the goggles she and Elara had been working on. It was clear that this workshop had once been a hub of innovation, where mages and techies had come together in their quest to bridge the two worlds.

As she delved deeper, Lila discovered projects that ranged from the rudimentary to the highly advanced. There were prototypes of flying machines powered by both tech and magic, enchanted armors that could adapt to their wearer's needs, and devices that could harness the energy of both realms.

But what caught Lila's attention the most was a series of journals, their pages yellowed with age. They bore the accounts of mages and techies who had once walked these halls, their dreams, aspirations, and the challenges they faced in their endeavors.

Lila sat down, her fingers flipping through the pages, absorbing the tales of triumphs and failures. She realized that she and her friends were not the first to tread this path. The academy had a rich history of pioneers who had dared to dream, to merge the worlds of magic and tech.

As she read, Lila felt a deep sense of connection to these past innovators. Their struggles, their hopes, and their vision resonated with her own journey. She realized that this workshop was not just a relic of the past but a testament to the enduring spirit of innovation.

With renewed determination, Lila decided to share her discovery with her friends. This workshop, with its wealth of knowledge and history, could be the key to their success. It was a reminder that they were part of a legacy, a continuum of dreamers who believed in the power of magic and tech.

As Lila exited the chamber, she made a silent vow to honor the legacy of those who had come before her. She would continue their work, pushing the boundaries of what was possible, and bridging the worlds of magic and tech.

Cedric's Hidden Lab

Lila's exploration of the concealed chamber was interrupted by a faint hum, a resonance that was distinctly different from the ambient magic she had grown accustomed to. Drawn to it, she followed the sound, which led her to a secluded corner of the chamber. Hidden behind a heavy velvet curtain was a door, slightly ajar, with a soft glow emanating from within.

Pushing the door open, Lila found herself in a room that was in stark contrast to the rest of the chamber. This was no relic of the past; it was a state-of-the-art lab, filled with a blend of magical artifacts and cutting-edge tech equipment. At the center of the room stood a large crystal, pulsating with energy, surrounded by intricate runes and circuitry.

As Lila took in the surroundings, she noticed a series of notes scattered across a workbench. The handwriting was meticulous, and the notes detailed various experiments, formulas, and spells. It was evident that someone had been working diligently, trying to harness a powerful ancient spell.

Before she could delve deeper, a voice interrupted her thoughts. "Impressive, isn't it?" Cedric stepped out from the shadows, his expression a mix of pride and defensiveness. Lila, taken aback, tried to mask her surprise. "Cedric, this is your lab?"

Cedric nodded, his gaze fixed on the pulsating crystal. "Yes, this is where I've been conducting my experiments. While others are content with mere integration, I aim for dominance. Magic, in its purest form, is superior, and I intend to prove it."

Lila, recalling the notes she had just glimpsed, ventured, "You're trying to harness an ancient spell?"

Cedric's eyes flashed with a mix of excitement and trepidation. "Yes, a spell that has been lost to time. My family's legacy speaks of it, a power that can overshadow any tech. But it's not just about power, Lila. It's about proving that magic, in its essence, is unparalleled."

Lila could sense the weight of expectation bearing down on Cedric. The pressure to uphold his family's legacy, the desire to prove himself, and the internal conflict of being in an academy that championed integration. "Cedric, why keep this a secret?"

He sighed, running a hand through his hair. "My family, the purists, they wouldn't understand. They see the academy's efforts as dilution, a betrayal of our magical heritage. But I needed to know, to test the limits, to see if the tales of old held any truth."

Lila approached the workbench, picking up a vial filled with a shimmering liquid. "And have you succeeded?"

Cedric hesitated, then admitted, "Not entirely. The spell is volatile, unpredictable. There have been... setbacks. But I'm close, Lila. I can feel it."

Lila, sensing the depth of Cedric's passion and the burden of his legacy, reached out, placing a reassuring hand on his arm. "Cedric, the path you've chosen is fraught with challenges. But remember, it's not just about proving magic's superiority. It's about understanding, about finding a balance."

Cedric looked at Lila, his defenses momentarily lowered. "I know, Lila. But the weight of my family's expectations, the legacy... it's overwhelming."

Lila nodded, understanding the complexities of Cedric's journey. "Just promise me one thing, Cedric. Whatever you discover, whatever path you choose, do it for the right reasons. Not just to prove a point, but to truly understand the essence of both magic and tech."

Cedric took a deep breath, his resolve strengthened. "I promise, Lila. And thank you."

As Lila exited the lab, she realized that the academy was not just a place of learning and innovation. It was a crucible, where beliefs were tested, legacies were upheld or challenged, and destinies were forged.

Antagonistic Faction's Origins

Lila, Elara, and Finn, having explored Cedric's hidden lab, ventured deeper into the concealed chamber. The air grew colder, and the walls seemed to echo with whispers of the past. In a dimly lit alcove, they stumbled upon a dusty old chest. Intrigued, Lila carefully opened it, revealing a collection of worn-out journals and scrolls.

Elara, with her innate sense of history, gently picked up one of the journals. "These are ancient," she murmured, her fingers tracing the faded emblem on the cover—a symbol that was all too familiar to them. It was the insignia of the antagonistic faction that opposed the merger of magic and tech.

As they began to read, the pages unveiled tales of a time when the academy was in its infancy. The journals detailed the formation of the faction, born out of a group of purist mages who believed that magic should remain untainted by the advancements of technology. They were led by a charismatic mage named Phineas, a visionary who foresaw the potential dangers of merging the two worlds.

Phineas's writings spoke of a significant event that solidified the faction's beliefs. A grand experiment had been conducted at the academy, aiming to create a device that could harness both magic and tech. However, the experiment went awry, leading to a catastrophic explosion that claimed many lives and left a part of the academy in ruins. This tragedy was a turning point, strengthening the resolve of Phineas and his followers. They believed that the disaster was a clear sign that magic and tech were never meant to intertwine.

The journals also introduced other key figures in the faction. There was Seraphina, a gifted mage with the ability to manipulate time, who believed that the natural order of things should not be disrupted. Then there was Orion, a scholar who penned essays on the sanctity of magic and its spiritual connection to the world. His writings argued that introducing tech into the magical realm would sever this sacred bond.

As Lila and her friends delved deeper, they discovered accounts of secret meetings, rallies, and protests organized by the faction. They learned of alliances forged with powerful families outside the academy, families that shared the faction's beliefs and provided them with resources and support.

One particular entry caught Lila's attention. It was a personal account written by a young mage named Elysia, who had lost her twin brother in the ill-fated experiment. Her grief-stricken words painted a vivid picture of the pain and loss experienced by many in the aftermath of the disaster. "The merger of magic and tech took away the only family I had," she wrote. "We must ensure that such a tragedy never befalls anyone again."

Elara, having read a similar account, looked up, her eyes filled with empathy. "These journals... they provide context. The faction's beliefs aren't just born out of resistance to change. They stem from genuine pain and loss."

Finn, ever the pragmatist, added, "It's essential to understand their perspective, even if we don't agree with it. Knowledge is power, and these journals give us insight into the faction's motivations."

Lila nodded, deep in thought. "It's a reminder that every story has multiple sides. While we believe in the potential of merging magic and tech, we must also acknowledge the risks and the sacrifices made in the past."

As they carefully packed away the journals, the trio realized that their discovery was more than just a historical account. It was a testament to the complexities of progress, the challenges of innovation, and the eternal struggle between tradition and change.

Elara's Caution

As the trio carefully packed away the journals, the weight of their discovery hung heavily in the air. The dimly lit chamber seemed to echo with the voices of the past, each tale a testament to the challenges of merging magic and tech.

Elara, her fingers still tracing the worn pages of the last journal, took a deep breath. "You know," she began, her voice soft, "these journals remind me of the tales my grandmother used to tell me."

Lila and Finn exchanged glances, sensing the gravity of Elara's words. They settled down on the cold stone floor, giving her their full attention.

"My grandmother was a historian," Elara continued, "and she had a vast collection of stories from the olden days. She often spoke of the 'Era of Trials,' a time when mages and inventors first attempted to merge magic and tech."

Lila leaned forward, her curiosity piqued. "What happened during this era?"

Elara's eyes took on a distant look. "Many things. Some wondrous, some tragic. There was a tale of an inventor named Aleron who created a device that could harness the power of the sun using magic. It was a marvel, providing light and warmth to entire villages. But one day, the device malfunctioned, causing a massive explosion. The village was destroyed, and many lives were lost."

Finn frowned. "That's terrible. But why did it malfunction?"

Elara sighed. "The device was ahead of its time. Aleron had successfully merged magic and tech, but he didn't fully understand the complexities and the balance required. The magic became unstable, leading to the disaster."

Lila looked thoughtful. "It's a cautionary tale, isn't it? About the dangers of pushing boundaries without understanding the consequences."

Elara nodded. "Exactly. And there were other tales too. Like the one about the 'Singing Stones.' These were magical stones that could produce beautiful melodies when infused with tech. But over time, the magic within the stones began to wane, and they lost their song forever."

Finn looked pensive. "So, the merger of magic and tech isn't just about creating something new. It's also about preserving the essence of what already exists."

"Yes," Elara agreed. "And that's why we need to tread carefully. The journals we found, the tales I've heard, they all serve as reminders of the challenges we face. We're on the brink of something incredible, but we must also be aware of the risks."

Lila took a deep breath, absorbing Elara's words. "We have the knowledge and the tools to make a difference. But we also have a responsibility to ensure that our actions don't lead to unintended consequences."

Elara smiled, placing a reassuring hand on Lila's shoulder. "That's the spirit. We learn from the past, but we also look to the future with hope and determination. Our journey won't be easy, but together, we can navigate the challenges and create a harmonious blend of magic and tech."

Finn nodded in agreement. "We have a unique opportunity to bridge two worlds. And with caution, understanding, and collaboration, we can achieve greatness."

The trio sat in silence for a moment, reflecting on their journey and the path ahead. The hidden chamber, with its remnants of the past, served as a poignant reminder of the academy's history and the legacy they were now a part of.

As they prepared to leave, Elara took one last look at the journals. "These stories, these lessons, they're a gift. And it's up to us to ensure that the next chapters we write are filled with hope, innovation, and a deep respect for the magic and tech that define our world."

With renewed determination, Lila, Elara, and Finn left the chamber, ready to face the challenges and opportunities that awaited them.

Chapter 6: The Tournament's Prelude and Ethical Debates

The grand hall of the academy was a spectacle of splendor and tradition, where the echoes of the past mingled with the whispers of the future. Majestic columns adorned with intricate carvings reached towards the vaulted ceiling, while the floor was a mosaic of magical runes and technological circuits, symbolizing the union of two worlds.

Students and faculty, dressed in their finest robes and attire, filled the hall, their faces glowing with anticipation. The chatter was a symphony of excitement, curiosity, and reverence, all awaiting the words of the Headmistress.

Standing tall on the elevated platform, the Headmistress, a figure of wisdom and grace, cleared her throat. Her eyes, twinkling with a knowing glimmer, scanned the crowd as he began to speak.

"Esteemed scholars, distinguished guests, and beloved students," she intoned, her voice resonating with authority and warmth. "Today, we stand on the threshold of a new era, an era that beckons us to transcend our limitations, to explore the uncharted, and to weave the fabric of our destiny."

A hush fell over the hall as he continued, "I am honored to announce the inception of the Grand Fairy-Tech Tournament, a celebration of our heritage, our innovation, and our unity."

The words hung in the air, imbued with significance and promise. The Headmistress's voice, rich and measured, painted a vivid picture of the tournament's grandeur.

"This tournament is not a mere competition," she emphasized, her eyes ablaze with conviction. "It is a journey, a quest for excellence, where magic and technology shall dance in harmony, where creativity shall blossom, and where the seeds of cooperation shall be sown."

She paused, allowing the profundity of his words to sink in. "In this hallowed hall, where the echoes of our ancestors resonate, we shall embark on a path that honors our traditions while embracing the new. We shall forge alliances, challenge paradigms, and ignite the spark of innovation."

The crowd was spellbound, entranced by the vision she had laid before them. The Headmistress's speech was not merely an announcement; it was a call to action, a rallying cry for the academy's brightest minds to unite in a common purpose.

"The Grand Fairy-Tech Tournament," she concluded, her voice softening, "is a testament to our belief in the power of collaboration, in the magic of discovery, and in the potential that lies within each one of us. Let us embark on this journey with courage, with curiosity, and with a commitment to excellence."

The hall erupted in applause, a thunderous affirmation of the Headmistress's words. The air was charged with energy, with dreams taking flight and possibilities unfolding. The tournament was no longer a mere event; it had become a symbol, a beacon of hope, and a promise of a future where magic and technology would thrive together in harmony.

The Headmistress's eyes met those of the students, a silent acknowledgment of the responsibility they now shared. The stage was set, the challenge was laid, and the academy was ready to write a new chapter in its storied history.

The Tournament Announcement had been made, and the adventure had begun.

The Mysterious Prize

As the applause for the Headmistress's speech began to wane, a hushed murmur of anticipation spread through the grand hall. The Headmistress, sensing the collective curiosity, raised a hand for silence.

"Now, onto the heart of the matter," she began, her voice dripping with intrigue. "The challenge that awaits our talented participants. Teams will be tasked with creating something truly groundbreaking: a device or spell that seamlessly merges the wonders of magic with the marvels of technology."

The hall was abuzz with whispers, the enormity of the task dawning on the students. The fusion of magic and tech was a frontier few had dared to tread, and the challenge promised to push the boundaries of their skills and imaginations.

"But what of the prize?" a bold voice called out from the crowd. All eyes turned to a young mage, her hand raised inquisitively.

The Headmistress smiled, a twinkle in her eye. "Ah, the prize. The reward for such a monumental achievement must be equally monumental, must it not?" She paused, letting the suspense build. "The prize for this tournament will remain... a mystery."

A collective gasp filled the room. Whispers turned into animated discussions as students and faculty alike speculated on what the prize could be. Was it a powerful artifact? A scholarship? A position of prestige within the academy? The possibilities were endless, and the mystery only added to the allure.

Lila leaned over to Finn, her eyes wide with excitement. "Can you imagine what it could be? It must be something truly extraordinary!"

Finn nodded, his mind racing. "Whatever it is, it's worth the challenge. We have to give it our all."

Elara, ever the pragmatist, chimed in, "Let's not get ahead of ourselves. The task at hand is daunting. We need to focus on that first."

Maya, lost in thought, mused aloud, "A prize so grand that they won't even reveal it? It's either something beyond our wildest dreams or a lesson in itself."

Across the hall, Cedric scoffed, "A mystery prize? Probably some gimmick to get us all invested. But no matter, my team will prevail, and the prize will be ours."

The faculty, too, were abuzz with speculation. Professor Eldrin, a staunch advocate for the integration of magic and tech, remarked to his colleague, "This is a brilliant move. The mystery will drive them, push them to innovate like never before."

Professor Lysandra, always skeptical, replied, "Or it could lead to disappointment. High stakes, Eldrin. I hope the academy knows what it's doing."

The Headmistress, observing the reactions, felt a surge of satisfaction. The mystery surrounding the prize had achieved its purpose: to ignite a fire of curiosity, determination, and excitement. The stage was set for a tournament unlike any other, where the journey and the unknown reward would be equally cherished.

The Mysterious Prize had set the academy abuzz, and the race to unravel its secrets had begun.

Team Dynamics

In the wake of the announcement, the grand hall of the academy transformed into a bustling hub of activity. Students huddled in groups, discussing strategies, potential teammates, and the mysterious prize. Amidst the chaos, Lila, with determined eyes, approached Finn, Elara, and Maya.

"We need a team," Lila began, her voice firm. "And I think the four of us have the perfect blend of skills."

Finn, with his tech-savvy mind and a penchant for tinkering, nodded in agreement. "I've been working on a device that could potentially merge magic and tech. But I need the right spellwork to make it functional."

Elara, a prodigious spellcaster with a vast knowledge of ancient magics, chimed in, "I've studied some old texts that might help. But we'll need someone who understands the essence of both worlds."

Maya, a scholar who had dedicated her life to the study of the convergence of magic and technology, smiled. "That's where I come in. I've been researching the harmonization of the two for years."

The formation of their team felt natural, almost destined. Lila, with her leadership skills and fierce determination, would drive the team forward. Finn's technical expertise, combined with Elara's magical prowess and Maya's deep understanding, made them a formidable force.

Across the hall, Cedric, with his tall stature and piercing blue eyes, gathered a group of like-minded individuals. They were purists, believing in the superiority of magic over technology. "We will show them the true power of pure magic," Cedric declared, his voice dripping with disdain for the tech enthusiasts.

His team consisted of Alaric, a master of elemental magic; Seraphina, known for her enchantments; and Orion, a strategist with a deep knowledge of magical history. They shared Cedric's views, believing that the integration of tech would dilute the essence of magic.

The dynamics within each team were starkly different. Lila's team thrived on collaboration, with each member respecting and valuing the others' expertise. They brainstormed, debated, and experimented, pushing each other to think outside the box. Their diverse backgrounds and skills were their strength, but they also posed challenges. Balancing the technical with the magical, ensuring that one didn't overpower the other, was a constant struggle.

Cedric's team, on the other hand, moved with singular focus. Their shared ideology made decision-making swift, but it also limited their perspective. They were exceptional in their magical abilities, but their disdain for technology could be their Achilles' heel.

As the days progressed, the academy watched with bated breath. The two teams, with their contrasting approaches, became the talk of the academy. Lila's team, with their innovative experiments, drew curious onlookers, eager to witness the fusion of magic and tech.

Cedric's team, with their powerful spells and enchantments, showcased the might of pure magic.

However, the journey wasn't without its challenges. Lila's team faced technical glitches, misaligned spells, and heated debates. But with each setback, they grew stronger, learning from their mistakes and adapting. Cedric's team, while powerful, struggled with the constraints of the challenge. Their purist approach limited their options, and they grappled with finding a way to stay true to their beliefs while meeting the requirements.

The dynamics within and between the teams set the stage for an epic showdown.

Ethical Debates

The grand hall of the academy, usually a place of celebration and unity, was now a cauldron of heated discussions and debates. The announcement of the tournament had ignited a firestorm of opinions, with the ethical implications of merging magic and technology at the heart of it all.

In one corner, a group of older students, who had witnessed the previous conflicts between magic and tech, voiced their concerns. "This tournament is a dangerous game," said one, a tall, dark-haired young man with a scar running down his cheek, a reminder of past battles. "We've seen the devastation when magic and tech clash. Do we really want to risk reigniting those flames?"

A young woman, her blue robes indicating her status as a scholar of magical history, added, "The ancient texts warn of the dangers of merging the two. The balance between magic and technology is delicate. This tournament could tip the scales, leading to unforeseen consequences."

However, not everyone shared these fears. A group of younger students, their eyes filled with excitement and wonder, saw the tournament as an opportunity. "Think of the possibilities!" exclaimed a bright-eyed first-year. "We could create spells that harness the power of technology, or devices that are enhanced by magic. The potential for innovation is limitless!"

Another chimed in, "The past conflicts were a result of ignorance and fear. We're more enlightened now. We understand the value of both magic and tech. This tournament is a chance to showcase that understanding and pave the way for a brighter future."

The debates weren't limited to the students. The faculty, too, was divided. Professor Althor, a staunch purist, believed that magic should remain untainted by technology. "Magic is pure, ancient, and sacred. Introducing technology into it is akin to polluting a pristine river. We must preserve the sanctity of our art," he argued.

On the other hand, Professor Lyria, a pioneer in the field of techno-magic, saw things differently. "Change is inevitable," she said, her voice calm and measured. "Instead of resisting it, we should embrace it. By merging magic and tech, we can push the boundaries of what's possible. This tournament is a step in the right direction."

The debates often became personal. Lila, given her background in both magic and tech, found herself at the center of many discussions. "You of all people should understand the dangers," Cedric told her one evening, his voice dripping with disdain. "Your family suffered during the last conflict. Do you really want to see history repeat itself?"

Lila, never one to back down, replied, "It's because of my family's history that I see the value in this tournament. We have a chance to rewrite the narrative, to show that magic and tech can coexist harmoniously. I won't let fear hold me back."

The ethical debates also led to introspection. Finn, as he worked on his device, often found himself questioning the morality of his actions. "Are we playing with fire?" he wondered aloud one night, as he and Elara pored over ancient texts.

Elara, looking up from a dusty tome, replied, "Every innovation comes with risks. But it also comes with rewards. We have to weigh the two and decide if the potential benefits outweigh the dangers."

Maya, with her deep understanding of the convergence of magic and technology, often played the role of mediator. "We need to find a middle ground," she said during one particularly heated debate. "Instead of focusing on what could go wrong, let's focus on what could go right. Let's use this tournament as an opportunity to learn, grow, and innovate."

As the days leading up to the tournament dwindled, the debates showed no signs of abating. The grand hall echoed with passionate arguments, heartfelt pleas, and fervent discussions. The ethical implications of the tournament had touched a nerve, forcing everyone to confront their beliefs, fears, and hopes.

The academy was divided, but one thing was clear – the tournament had already achieved one of its objectives. It had sparked a dialogue, forcing everyone to think deeply about the role of magic and technology in their lives. Whether the tournament would lead to innovation or disaster remained to be seen, but it had undoubtedly set the stage for a pivotal moment in the academy's history.

Chapter 7: Preparations, Sabotage, and Personal Histories

The sun cast a golden hue over the Fairy-Tech Academy, its rays filtering through the tall, arched windows of the brainstorming room. Lila, Finn, Elara, and Maya sat around a large wooden table, strewn with scrolls, gadgets, and ancient tomes. The upcoming tournament weighed heavily on their minds, and the room buzzed with anticipation.

Lila began, her voice firm, "We need something groundbreaking, a blend of magic and tech that's never been seen before." She sketched a rough design on a piece of parchment, her fingers moving with precision.

Finn, always the tech enthusiast, pulled out a small device. "I've been working on this," he said, holding up a shimmering gadget that seemed to pulse with energy. "It's a tech core that can channel magical energy. If we can integrate this with a spell, it could revolutionize the way magic-tech works."

Elara's eyes sparkled with excitement. "That's brilliant, Finn! And I think I have just the spell." She unfurled an ancient scroll, revealing intricate symbols and runes. "This is a containment spell from the old world. If we can modify it to work with your tech core, we could create a device amplifies their powers."

Maya, ever the mediator, pondered aloud, "The key is balance. We can't let the tech overpower the magic or vice versa. It has to be a perfect blend, a harmony." She began drawing patterns, merging the tech designs with magical runes, creating a blueprint that was both ancient and futuristic.

The hours flew by as the team delved deep into their brainstorming session. Lila's leadership, Finn's tech innovations, Elara's magical prowess, and Maya's analytical skills combined to create a strategy that was both innovative and rooted in the academy's history. The synergy between magic and tech was evident in every design, every spell, and every idea they discussed.

As night fell, the room was illuminated by floating orbs of light, a blend of tech-powered bulbs and magical luminescence. The team looked at their combined efforts with pride, confident in their innovative strategies for the tournament.

Their unity and shared vision were palpable. They were not just merging magic and tech; they were merging their strengths, their histories, and their hopes for a brighter future.

Sabotage Strikes

The days following the brainstorming session were filled with a flurry of activity. Lila's team was hard at work in various locations within the academy, each member focused on their part of the project. The excitement was palpable, but so was the pressure. The tournament was drawing near, and they knew that their innovative approach would either dazzle the judges or fall flat.

Finn was the first to notice something amiss. While working late in the tech lab, he found that the tech core he had been developing was behaving erratically. At first, he attributed it to a miscalculation on his part, but as he delved deeper, he discovered that the core's programming had been tampered with.

"What's going on here?" he muttered to himself, his brow furrowed in concentration. The code was subtle, almost invisible, but it was there—a deliberate attempt to sabotage his work.

Meanwhile, Elara was facing her own challenges. The ancient spell she had chosen was reacting unpredictably when she tried to integrate it with modern technology. It was as if the magic itself was resisting the merger. But upon closer inspection, she found signs of interference in the magical flow, a disruption that seemed intentional.

The setbacks continued to mount. Maya's analytical models were producing inconsistent results, and Lila's designs were inexplicably flawed. Doubt began to creep into their minds. Was their approach fundamentally wrong? Or was something more sinister at play?

The team convened in their brainstorming room, the excitement now replaced with tension and suspicion.

"Someone's trying to sabotage us," Finn declared, his voice filled with frustration.

"It's not just the tech," Elara added, her eyes wide with realization. "The magic has been tampered with as well."

Lila's mind raced. Who would want to sabotage them? And why? The answer was both obvious and unsettling. The antagonistic faction had made their opposition to the merger of magic and tech clear. But would they go so far as to sabotage their efforts?

"We need to investigate," Maya said, her voice calm but determined. "We can't let them derail our project."

The team split up, each member following leads, probing for evidence, and trying to uncover the truth behind the sabotage. The once vibrant academy now seemed filled with shadows and whispers. Friends were eyed with suspicion, and every setback was a potential act of sabotage.

As the days wore on, the evidence began to point unmistakably towards the antagonistic faction. Lila found traces of their involvement in the tampered designs, and Finn discovered connections between the sabotaged tech core and known members of the faction.

The suspense was unbearable. The once united academy was now a battleground of ideologies, and Lila's team was caught in the crossfire. The stakes were high, and the tension was palpable. The readers would be on the edge of their seats, eager to find out who was behind the sabotage and what their motivations were.

But amidst the chaos and suspicion, the team's resolve only strengthened. They knew that their innovative approach was not just a tournament entry but a symbol of a future where magic and tech could coexist. They would not be deterred, and they would not be defeated.

The stage was set for a confrontation, a clash of ideals and a test of their determination. The sabotage had struck, but it had not broken them. The tournament loomed, and they were ready to face it, united and undeterred.

Lila and Cedric's Clash

The academy's grand hall, with its towering marble pillars and intricate mosaics, was a testament to the rich history of magic. On any other day, it echoed with laughter and the hum of spells being practiced. But today, it was the backdrop for a confrontation that had the entire academy on edge.

Lila, her sun-kissed hair cascading down her back, stood with her team behind her. They were a diverse group, each representing a different facet of the academy's teachings. Opposite them, Cedric, with his sharp features and piercing blue eyes, stood tall. His followers, loyal to the core, flanked him, their expressions a mix of defiance and concern.

"Why are you doing this, Cedric?" Lila began, her voice echoing in the vast hall. "We're on the cusp of something revolutionary. A blend of magic and technology that could change the world. Why can't you see the potential?"

Cedric's gaze was unwavering. "It's not about potential, Lila. It's about tradition, about respecting the boundaries set by our ancestors."

Lila's green eyes flashed with frustration. "We're not erasing tradition. We're building upon it. Evolving."

Cedric's voice grew louder, more passionate. "At what cost? My family learned the hard way about meddling with forces beyond our understanding. The explosion... the lives lost... all because of a reckless pursuit of power."

A murmur ran through Lila's team. They had heard whispers of the tragedy that had befallen Cedric's family, but hearing it from him gave it a weight they couldn't ignore.

Lila's voice softened. "I'm truly sorry for your family's loss, Cedric. But we've come a long way since then. We have checks and balances, safety measures..."

Cedric cut her off, his voice trembling with emotion. "Safety measures? Is that what you call them? My sister, Elise, was part of your experiments. She hasn't been the same since."

Lila's face paled. She had known Elise was involved, but she hadn't realized the extent of the impact. "Cedric, I..."

Cedric took a step forward, his eyes blazing. "You play with forces you don't fully understand, Lila. And people get hurt. My family has paid the price once. I won't let it happen again."

The two stood there, the weight of their histories and beliefs creating a chasm between them. The hall, filled with students and faculty, was silent, each person lost in their thoughts, grappling with the complexities of progress and tradition.

Finally, Lila spoke, her voice filled with conviction. "Cedric, we can't let fear hold us back. We have a responsibility to push boundaries, to explore new frontiers. But we also have a duty to do it safely, responsibly. Let's work together, find a middle ground."

Cedric looked at her, his expression softening. "I want to believe it's possible, Lila. But the scars of the past run deep."

Lila reached out, touching his arm gently. "Then let's heal those scars, together."

As the two leaders stood there, a fragile truce forming between them, the academy watched, hopeful for a future where magic and technology could coexist in harmony.

The meeting adjourned, but the tension lingered. Lila's team gathered around her, offering support and encouragement. Cedric's followers did the same, their loyalty to their leader evident in their words and actions.

Days turned into weeks, and the academy buzzed with activity. Lila and Cedric's clash had ignited a debate that spread like wildfire. Students and faculty alike were divided, some championing the integration of magic and technology, while others clung to tradition, fearful of the unknown.

Lila and Cedric continued to meet, their discussions intense and often heated. But slowly, understanding began to grow. Cedric shared more about his family's tragic past, the mistakes that had been made, and the lessons learned. Lila, in turn, opened up about her vision for the future, her belief in the power of innovation, and her commitment to doing things right.

They challenged each other, pushed each other to think deeper, to see beyond their own perspectives. And in doing so, they found common ground.

The academy watched, hopeful and inspired, as two strong leaders worked through their differences, forging a path toward a future that honored both tradition and innovation.

In the end, Lila and Cedric's clash was more than just a disagreement. It was a catalyst for change, a turning point that would shape the academy's future and leave a lasting impact on all who witnessed it. It was a reminder that progress and tradition need not be at odds, that with empathy, understanding, and collaboration, even the deepest divides can be bridged.

Character Insights

The sun had set, casting the academy in a soft, golden hue. Students bustled about, but in a quiet corner of the academy's vast gardens, two figures sat on an ornate stone bench, engrossed in conversation. Finn, with his tousled brown hair and glasses reflecting the last rays of the sun, looked at Maya, her dark eyes filled with curiosity.

"You know, Maya," Finn began, adjusting his glasses, "I wasn't always this passionate about tech. It was an incident from my childhood that set me on this path."

Maya leaned in, intrigued. "What happened?"

Finn took a deep breath, his eyes distant. "I was about ten. My family lived near a forest, and I'd often wander off, exploring. One day, I stumbled upon an old, abandoned house. Curiosity got the better of me, and I went in. The place was filled with relics from a bygone era, but what caught my eye was an old, rusted machine. I tinkered with it, and to my surprise, it came to life."

Maya's eyes widened. "What was it?"

Finn chuckled, "An old radio. But to me, it was magic. The voices, the music—it was like a portal to another world. That's when I realized the power of technology, how it could bridge gaps, connect people. I decided then that I wanted to be a part of that world, to create, innovate, and make a difference."

Maya smiled, touched by Finn's story. "It's amazing how certain moments can shape our lives. Speaking of which, I have a tale of my own."

Finn looked at her expectantly. "Do tell."

Maya took a moment, gathering her thoughts. "Centuries ago, my ancestors were known as the 'Peacekeepers.' They were powerful mages, but their true strength lay in their ability to mediate conflicts. During a particularly tumultuous period, when magic clans were at war, it was my ancestors who stepped in, risking their lives to broker peace."

Finn listened intently, captivated. "That's incredible. It must've taken immense courage."

Maya nodded. "It did. But they believed in a greater good. There's a particular story that's been passed down through generations. One of my ancestors, Aria, was faced with a near-impossible task. Two clans, both equally powerful, were on the brink of a catastrophic war. Aria, using her unique mediation magic, brought the leaders of both clans together. She made them see the bigger picture, the devastation their feud would bring."

"How did she do it?" Finn asked, genuinely curious.

Maya's eyes sparkled with pride. "She created a vision, a glimpse into the future, showing them the consequences of their actions—the destruction, the loss. It was a powerful, emotional experience, and it worked. The clans set aside their differences, forging an alliance that lasted generations."

Finn was silent for a moment, processing the story. "It's no wonder you're so good at bringing people together, Maya. It's in your blood."

Maya laughed, "Perhaps. But it's also a reminder of the responsibility we carry, the legacy we must uphold."

The two sat in companionable silence, lost in their thoughts. The stories they'd shared provided a deeper understanding of each other, strengthening the bond between them. As the stars began to twinkle overhead, Finn and Maya knew that their tales were not just about the past but also a beacon for the future, guiding them on their journey at the academy and beyond.

Chapter 8: The Tournament's Triumphs and Trials

The Fairy-Tech Academy's grand arena, a marvel of architectural brilliance, stood bathed in a soft, ethereal glow. Its towering walls, etched with ancient runes, whispered tales of bygone eras, while the state-of-the-art holographic systems hinted at a future full of promise. Today, this arena was not just a battleground for duels or a stage for debates; it was a vessel holding centuries of history, innovation, and dreams.

A reverent silence enveloped the gathered assembly. Students from various factions, faculty members adorned in their ceremonial robes, and distinguished guests from distant realms—all waited with bated breath. The air was thick with anticipation, each heartbeat echoing the legacy of the academy.

From the group of Elders, a distinguished figure stepped forward. It was Elder Magus, a beacon of wisdom whose tales of valor and vision were known to every pupil, including young Cedric. The Elder's robe, a mosaic of shimmering threads, seemed to capture the very essence of the academy's journey, from its humble beginnings to its current glory.

Clearing his throat, Elder Magus began, his voice resonating with the weight of history. "At the genesis of our realm, when magic was as wild as the roaring rivers and technology was but a distant star in the night sky, a dream was conceived. A dream of a sanctuary where the ancient art of magic and the budding promise of technology could thrive side by side. From that dream, the Fairy-Tech Academy emerged."

The audience was transported back in time as a holographic display painted the skies above. Scenes of the academy's early days came to life: visionaries laying the foundation stones, young mages and tech enthusiasts collaborating on their first projects, and the joyous celebrations of their initial successes.

Elder Magus continued, his tone shifting to reflect the highs and lows of their journey. "Our academy, over the eons, has been a lighthouse of progress. We've witnessed moments where magic and technology danced together, crafting marvels that reshaped our very existence. But, like any epic tale, our story too has its share of shadows."

The holographs now depicted darker times. Periods when unchecked ambitions led to experiments gone awry, casting doubts over the academy's principles. Scenes of magical explosions disrupting tech circuits and machines malfunctioning in the presence of certain spells served as somber reminders of their past mistakes.

Yet, as Elder Magus's narrative unfolded, it was evident that the academy's spirit was unyielding. "Each challenge," he emphasized, "only strengthened our resolve. It taught us the importance of balance, of understanding, and of collaboration."

His gaze, sharp and discerning, momentarily settled on Lila and her comrades. "This tournament is not merely a test of skills. It's a homage to our past, a celebration of our present, and a beacon for our future. We stand at the crossroads of history, and it is up to our young visionaries to guide us forward, to ensure that the dance between magic and technology continues harmoniously."

As Elder Magus concluded, the arena resonated with the sound of applause. The past had been honored, the present acknowledged, and the future entrusted to the next generation. The stage was now set for the young innovators to take the spotlight, and the audience, having been reminded of the academy's storied past, was eager to glimpse the future.

Lila's Team's Innovation

As teams from various factions prepared their presentations, there was a palpable sense of competition in the air. Each group hoped to unveil an innovation that would leave a mark, but the buzz was especially loud about Lila's team. Rumors had spread about their groundbreaking approach, and the audience was eager to witness it firsthand.

Lila, with her long hair tied back and her enchanted goggles resting on her forehead, took a deep breath as she stepped onto the stage. The arena's vastness could be intimidating, but she felt the reassuring presence of her team behind her.

"Honored judges, esteemed guests, and fellow innovators," Lila began, her voice echoing with clarity and confidence, "Today, we stand before you not just as representatives of our respective fields, but as ambassadors of a vision. A vision where magic and technology coexist, not as rivals, but as partners."

Behind her, a large holographic screen came to life, displaying intricate blueprints of their creation. It was a device that seemed to be born from the heart of both an ancient spellbook and a futuristic tech lab. "Introducing the 'MagiTech Harmonizer'," Lila announced, "A beacon of integration, designed to channel magical energies seamlessly into technological circuits, ensuring operations that are both efficient and harmonious."

Elara, her violet eyes shimmering with passion, stepped forward. With a graceful gesture, she summoned a miniature model of the Harmonizer, which floated gently in the air beside her. "Magic, in its essence, is the energy of the universe," she explained. "Our Harmonizer is designed to tap into this vast reservoir, channeling elemental forces like water, wind, and fire into tech devices without any disruption or energy wastage."

Finn, his steel-gray eyes twinkling with mischief, took over the stage with his signature flair. "Now, for the tech enthusiasts among us," he began, drawing chuckles from the audience, "The Harmonizer isn't just about flashy magic. Its circuitry, crafted with precision and innovation, ensures compatibility with a range of devices. From your everyday gadgets to advanced machinery, this device bridges the gap."

Maya, always the analytical mind, presented a series of holographic charts and graphs. "Data doesn't lie," she stated confidently. "Our tests show a significant increase in efficiency levels when using the Harmonizer. Moreover, the potential applications in sectors like healthcare, transportation, and energy are limitless."

The audience was spellbound. Whispers of admiration spread like wildfire. It was evident that Lila's team had achieved something extraordinary. They had not merely merged magic and tech; they had created a symphony, a dance of energies that complemented and elevated each other.

As their presentation drew to a close, a thunderous applause filled the arena. Judges, including the venerable Professor Eldrin, exchanged nods of approval. It was clear that the Fairy-Tech Academy had witnessed a defining moment in its illustrious history.

The Harmonizer was more than a device; it was a symbol. A symbol of unity, innovation, and the boundless possibilities that awaited when two worlds, often seen in contrast, came together in harmony.

Challenges Arise

Whispers filled the vast space of the grand arena as students and faculty alike awaited the next presentation. Lila's team had just showcased their groundbreaking approach, blending magic and tech seamlessly. The applause had barely died down when the first signs of trouble began.

A sudden power outage plunged the arena into darkness. Panic ensued as students scrambled, trying to figure out what had happened. The massive holographic screens that displayed the team's innovations flickered and went blank. Lila's heart raced. She knew this wasn't a mere technical glitch. The timing was too convenient.

From the shadows, murmurs arose, hinting at sabotage. The antagonistic faction, known for their staunch opposition to the merging of magic and tech, were prime suspects. They had been vocal about their disapproval, but resorting to such measures was unprecedented.

Lila gathered her team. "We need to stay calm," she urged, her voice steady despite the chaos around them. "Elara, can you use your elemental magic to create some light?"

Elara nodded, summoning a soft luminescent orb that floated above them, casting a gentle glow. The sight of the magical illumination amidst the tech-heavy environment was a stark reminder of the balance they were striving for.

Finn, ever the problem-solver, was already on his knees, examining the main power console. "It's not just a power cut," he announced grimly. "Someone's tampered with the system. There's a magical residue here, mixed with some kind of tech interference."

Maya, with her analytical prowess, joined Finn. "Let me see if I can trace the source," she said, her fingers dancing over the console. Her pendant, half gear and half crystal, glowed intermittently as she worked.

The audience watched, their initial panic turning into anticipation. Here was real-time proof of Lila's team's ability to handle crises, merging magic and tech under pressure.

After what felt like hours but was only minutes, Maya looked up. "Got it!" she exclaimed. "It's a dual-layered sabotage. A tech virus introduced into the system, masked and protected by a magical barrier."

Lila's eyes narrowed. "Can we counter it?"

Maya nodded. "With Finn's tech expertise and Elara's magic, we can. But we need to work together."

The next moments were a blur of activity. Elara chanted incantations, her hands moving in intricate patterns, while Finn, with his tech gauntlet, typed furiously, bypassing corrupted systems and isolating the virus. Maya coordinated their efforts, her analytical mind finding the most efficient way to merge their skills.

The audience was spellbound. The very essence of the academy's ethos was unfolding before them—magic and tech, working in harmony.

With a final combined effort, power surged back. The screens lit up, brighter and clearer than before. The arena erupted in applause, not just for the team's initial presentation but for their resilience and innovation in the face of adversity.

However, the sabotage had revealed the deep-seated tensions within the academy. The challenges Lila's team faced were not just technical or magical; they were ideological. The incident was a stark reminder that while they had made significant strides in merging magic and tech, the journey was far from over.

As the applause continued, Lila's gaze swept the arena, finally resting on Cedric. His expression was inscrutable, but there was a hint of admiration in his eyes. The events of the day had tested Lila's team but also also sown the seeds of change in those who had once opposed them.

Chapter 9: Unraveling Tensions and the Quest for Unity

The applause for Lila's team was still echoing through the grand arena when a sudden, chilling silence descended. From the shadows, a group of individuals stepped forward, their expressions stern and their intentions clear. They were members of the antagonistic faction, and they had come with a purpose.

Led by Alaric, a tall, imposing figure with a silver streak running through his raven-black hair, the faction members positioned themselves between Lila's team and their audience. Alaric raised his hand, and the arena's ambient lights dimmed, replaced by a spotlight that focused solely on him.

"Esteemed members of the Fairy-Tech Academy," Alaric began, his voice dripping with disdain, "What you've just witnessed is a dangerous delusion. The merging of magic and tech, as presented, is not the salvation we seek but the very doom that awaits us."

He gestured to his side, and another faction member, a woman with piercing blue eyes named Seraphina, unveiled a device. It was starkly different from Lila's creation. Cold, metallic, and devoid of any magical aura, it stood as a testament to the faction's belief in the separation of magic and tech.

"This," Alaric declared, "is the true path forward. A device designed to keep magic and tech apart, ensuring that their volatile energies never intersect. Only by keeping them separate can we prevent the catastrophes of the past from revisiting us."

Murmurs of confusion and concern rippled through the audience. Many remembered the tales of the great war, of the devastation caused when magic and tech collided uncontrollably. But Lila's presentation had offered hope, a vision of a harmonious future. Alaric's interruption was a stark reminder of the deep divisions that still existed within the academy.

Seraphina stepped forward, activating the device. A barrier of energy emanated from it, pushing away any magical essence in its vicinity. Simultaneously, a series of mechanical arms extended, each interfacing with various technological platforms but ensuring that no magical interference occurred.

"The future lies in understanding and respecting the boundaries of both magic and tech," Seraphina explained. "Our device ensures that each domain remains pure, untainted by the other. This is the only way to guarantee our safety and the continued prosperity of our world."

The tension in the arena was palpable. Students, faculty, and guests were torn. While many were swayed by the faction's arguments, recalling the horrors of the past, others believed in the vision presented by Lila's team, a future where magic and tech coexisted in harmony.

Lila, not one to be easily deterred, stepped forward, her gaze locked onto Alaric's. "While we respect your perspective," she began, her voice steady, "we believe in a world where magic and tech can complement each other. Our device is not just a piece of innovation; it's a symbol of hope, of unity, and of progress."

Alaric smirked, "Hope is a dangerous thing, especially when it blinds you to reality."

The stage was set for a showdown, not just of devices and ideologies but of beliefs and visions for the future. The Fairy-Tech Academy, a place of learning and innovation, was now at the epicenter of a debate that would shape its destiny and that of the world beyond.

Historical Ties

The grand arena, once filled with the buzz of excitement and innovation, now held a somber atmosphere. The Faction's disruption had left many in shock, but it was the presence of Elder Thrain, one of the oldest members of the antagonistic faction, that commanded everyone's attention. His age was evident, with deep wrinkles etching his face and silver hair cascading down his back, but his eyes held a fire that belied his years.

Elder Thrain stepped forward, his staff tapping rhythmically against the stone floor. "Many of you," he began, his voice quivering but strong, "may wonder why we, the older generation, harbor such distrust towards the merging of magic and tech. Today, I will share a tale, a personal one, that might shed light on our reservations."

He paused, taking a deep breath, as if gathering strength for the memories he was about to relive. "The great war, as many of you have read in your history books, was a time of chaos and devastation. But what the books don't tell you are the personal stories, the families torn apart, the lives lost in the blink of an eye."

A hush fell over the audience, every eye fixed on the elder. "I had a brother," Thrain continued, "A brilliant mage named Elthor. He believed, much like many of you today, in the potential of merging magic and tech. He worked tirelessly, crafting devices that could harness the power of both. And for a time, it seemed he had succeeded."

Thrain's eyes misted over, lost in the memories. "But one fateful day, an experiment went awry. The energies of magic and tech, instead of merging, clashed violently. The explosion decimated our family home, taking with it my dear brother and many others."

The weight of his words hung heavily in the air. "Many families suffered similar fates. Among them were the ancestors of young Cedric." Thrain gestured towards Cedric, who sat, head bowed, absorbing the gravity of his family's history.

"The aftermath of the war left deep scars, not just on the land but in our hearts. We vowed never to let such a catastrophe happen again. And so, we formed this faction, not out of malice, but out of a desire to protect future generations from the mistakes of the past."

Thrain looked around the arena, his gaze piercing. "It is not distrust in innovation that drives us, but the painful memories of lost loved ones. We wish to prevent history from repeating itself, to ensure that no more lives are lost in the pursuit of unchecked progress."

The elder's words resonated with many in the audience. While they might not agree with the faction's methods, they could no longer deny the depth of their convictions.

Lila, ever the diplomat, approached Elder Thrain. "Your story is a reminder of the weight of our responsibilities," she said softly. "While we strive for progress, we must also remember the lessons of the past. Perhaps, together, we can find a way to move forward without forgetting where we came from."

Elder Thrain nodded, a hint of a smile playing on his lips. "Perhaps, young one. Perhaps."

The arena, once divided by clashing ideologies, now held a sense of unity. The path ahead was uncertain, but with understanding and collaboration, there was hope for a brighter future.

The Academy's Challenge

The grand arena, which had witnessed moments of innovation, disruption, and heartfelt revelations, was about to undergo its most dramatic transformation yet. As the last words of Elder Thrain's story faded, a deep rumble echoed throughout the space. The ground trembled, and the vast expanse of the arena began to shift and morph.

Before the eyes of the astounded audience, the flat surface of the arena cracked and split, giving way to towering walls and intricate pathways. Stone and metal intertwined with vines and glowing runes, creating a sprawling labyrinth that stretched out in all directions. The once open arena was now a maze of challenges, each section radiating a unique aura of magic and tech.

A holographic projection of Headmistress Elowen appeared above the labyrinth. "Students," her voice boomed, "this is the Academy's Challenge. A test of your skills, wit, and the harmony between magic and tech. Your task is to navigate this labyrinth, overcoming the obstacles and puzzles that lie within. Remember, this is not just a test of individual prowess but of teamwork and collaboration."

Lila, Elara, Maya, and their teammates exchanged determined glances. They had faced numerous challenges leading up to this moment, and they were ready to tackle this one head-on. With a nod from Lila, the team entered the labyrinth.

The first section they encountered was a forest of metal trees, their branches adorned with glowing crystals. As they ventured deeper, the trees began to move, their branches reaching out to block their path. Elara, tapping into her magical heritage, whispered an incantation, causing the trees to sway in rhythm, creating a synchronized dance that allowed the team to pass.

Further ahead, they came across a vast chasm. A series of floating platforms, some stable and others phasing in and out of existence, were the only means of crossing. Maya's analytical skills shone as she quickly deciphered the pattern of the platforms. Guiding her team, they leaped from one platform to the next, their trust in Maya's calculations unwavering.

As they progressed, the challenges grew more complex. In one section, they faced a series of mirrors that reflected distorted versions of reality. Using a combination of tech gadgets and illusion-breaking spells, they navigated the deceptive maze.

In another area, they encountered a massive golem, powered by both magic and machinery. Instead of confronting it head-on, the team combined their skills to reprogram and pacify the creature, turning a potential threat into an ally.

Throughout the labyrinth, the unity of Lila's team was evident. They complemented each other's strengths and compensated for each other's weaknesses. Their approach to each challenge, seamlessly merging magic and tech, was a testament to their growth and understanding.

However, the labyrinth had one final test in store. The team reached a vast chamber, at the center of which stood a pedestal holding a crystal orb. Surrounding the pedestal was a complex array of runes and tech circuits, a puzzle that required both magical and technological expertise to solve.

Lila took the lead, her fingers dancing over the runes as she channeled her magic. Elara and Maya worked in tandem, the former manipulating the magical elements while the latter adjusted the tech components. The rest of the team provided support, offering insights and solutions.

After what felt like hours, a harmonious hum filled the chamber. The runes and circuits glowed brightly, and the crystal orb levitated, emitting a radiant light. The puzzle was solved, and the labyrinth's final challenge was overcome.

As the team exited the labyrinth, they were met with thunderous applause. The audience, which included students, faculty, and even members of the antagonistic faction, were on their feet, their faces reflecting a mix of awe and respect.

Headmistress Elowen approached Lila's team, a proud smile on her face. "Congratulations," she said. "You have navigated the Academy's Challenge and have also demonstrated the true potential of merging magic and tech. Your journey through the labyrinth will be remembered for generations to come."

The team, exhausted but elated, shared a group hug. They had faced the Academy's Challenge and emerged victorious, their bond stronger than ever.

Chapter 10: Labyrinth Trials, Collaborations, and Realizations

The transformed arena was a marvel to behold. Towering walls, shifting pathways, and zones pulsating with both magical and technological energy created a maze that was both daunting and awe-inspiring. The labyrinth was designed not just to challenge the students' skills but also their ability to adapt, collaborate, and think outside the box.

Lila, with her team by her side, took a deep breath as they entered the first zone. She adjusted her goggles, a piece of tech she had personally enhanced with both magical and technological components. The lenses flickered for a moment before displaying a holographic overlay of the labyrinth's layout. The goggles could decipher patterns, detect magical anomalies, and even suggest possible solutions to tech-based puzzles.

As they ventured deeper, they encountered their first challenge: a room filled with floating platforms, each inscribed with runes that emitted a soft glow. The challenge was to activate the runes in a specific sequence to create a bridge across. Lila's goggles analyzed the patterns, and with a few calculated jumps and rune activations, the team successfully navigated the room.

However, the labyrinth was not just about individual challenges. In the next zone, they were joined by another team, one that included members of the antagonistic faction. The room was divided into two sections, one brimming with tech components and the other radiating magical energy. To proceed, both teams had to work together, combining their expertise.

At first, the atmosphere was tense. Old rivalries and disagreements threatened to hinder their progress. But as minutes turned into hours, the urgency of the situation forced them to set aside their differences.

Lila, taking the lead, coordinated the efforts, ensuring that both magic and tech were utilized effectively.

In one memorable challenge, a massive door blocked their path. The door had two locks: one that required a magical key and the other a technological code. Lila's team focused on the magical aspect, channeling their energies to conjure the key, while members of the antagonistic faction worked on deciphering the code. The moment the door swung open, marking their collaborative success, was met with cheers and sighs of relief from both teams.

The labyrinth also had its share of surprises. In one zone, the floor suddenly gave way, leading to a slide that transported the students to an underground chamber filled with luminescent mushrooms and tech drones. Here, the challenge was to collect specific mushrooms while avoiding the drones. Lila's goggles proved invaluable, highlighting the required mushrooms and predicting the drones' flight patterns.

As they navigated challenge after challenge, something remarkable happened. The students began to bond. Shared moments of triumph, laughter at unexpected mishaps, and collective brainstorming sessions blurred the lines between teams and factions. By the time they reached the final zone, a sense of camaraderie had developed.

The last challenge was the most complex. A giant crystal stood at the center of the room, surrounded by a network of beams, mirrors, and magical barriers. The objective was to direct a beam of light, infused with both magic and tech, towards the crystal. It required precise calculations, magical enhancements, and impeccable timing. Lila, with her goggles providing real-time feedback, orchestrated the team's efforts. After several attempts, the beam hit the crystal, filling the room with a radiant glow and signaling their success.

Exhausted but exhilarated, the students exited the labyrinth. They both overcame intricate challenges and forged unexpected alliances and friendships.

As Lila removed her goggles, she looked around at the smiling faces of her teammates and the members of the antagonistic faction. The labyrinth had taught them a valuable lesson: when magic and tech come together, and when individuals collaborate despite their differences, anything is possible

***

The labyrinth's challenges had tested the students' mettle, pushing them to their limits. But as they ventured deeper into the maze, the trials became even more intricate, demanding a seamless blend of magic and technology.

Finn, with his tech-savvy background, took the lead in one of the zones. The room was filled with a chaotic whirl of magical energy, swirling around and threatening to destabilize the entire area. The source of the disturbance was a magical anomaly, a vortex of raw, uncontrolled power. Most students would have been overwhelmed, but Finn saw it as an opportunity.

Drawing from his tech knowledge, Finn quickly assembled a makeshift stabilizer from the various components scattered around the room. Using principles of magnetic containment, he aimed to create a field that would contain and neutralize the magical vortex. As he worked, his fingers moved with precision, connecting wires, calibrating settings, and infusing the device with a touch of his own magic. When he activated the stabilizer, the room held its breath. Slowly, the chaotic energy began to calm, drawn towards the stabilizer and neutralized. The vortex dissipated, leaving behind an aura of calm. Finn's triumph was a testament to the power of technology when applied with understanding and innovation.

But the labyrinth was not done. The next challenge was a vast chamber filled with holographic displays, each showing complex patterns and sequences. These were tech-based puzzles, but with a twist. To solve them, one needed to understand the underlying magical signatures.

Elara and Maya stepped forward. Elara, with her deep-rooted magical heritage, began to chant, her voice echoing through the chamber. As she did, the patterns on the displays began to shift, revealing hidden layers infused with magic. Maya, with her analytical mind, started to decipher the sequences, drawing connections between the tech patterns and their magical counterparts.

Together, they tackled each display. Elara would use her magic to reveal the hidden layers, while Maya would analyze and solve the sequence. One by one, the displays lit up with a soft green glow, signaling their successful completion. It was a dance of intellect and intuition, showcasing the harmony between magic and tech.

In one memorable moment, a particularly complex puzzle stumped the duo. The display showed a constantly shifting pattern, with layers of magic that seemed to contradict each other. But Elara and Maya were undeterred. They combined their strengths, with Elara channeling a spell to stabilize the magical layers while Maya used her tech knowledge to create a temporary algorithm that predicted the pattern's shifts. Working in tandem, they cracked the sequence, earning applause and admiration from their peers.

Their success in the chamber was more than just a triumph over the challenges. It was a statement, a demonstration of the potential that lay in the integration of magic and technology. Where magic brought intuition, emotion, and raw power, technology offered precision, logic, and innovation. Together, they were unstoppable.

As the students exited the chamber, there was a palpable sense of pride and accomplishment. They had faced some of the most demanding trials the academy had to offer and had emerged victorious. But more importantly, they had showcased the power of collaboration, proving that when magic and tech came together, the possibilities were endless.

In the midst of the labyrinth's challenges, Lila found herself in a secluded alcove, a brief respite from the trials. The dimly lit space was adorned with ancient runes and holographic displays, a testament to the academy's blend of magic and tech. As she caught her breath, a shadowy figure stepped into the alcove. It was Alaric, a senior member of the antagonistic faction, known for his staunch opposition to the merging of magic and tech.

Lila tensed, ready for a confrontation. But Alaric's demeanor was not hostile. Instead, he looked weary, the weight of years and burdens evident in his eyes. "Lila," he began, his voice soft, "I've watched you and your team. You're different."

Lila, taken aback, replied cautiously, "Different how?"

Alaric sighed, "You genuinely believe in the harmony of magic and tech. It's not just about winning the tournament for you. It's about a vision for the future."

Lila nodded, "It's a future I believe in. But why are you telling me this?"

Alaric hesitated, then said, "I want you to understand our perspective. The world wasn't always like this. There was a time when magic and tech were at odds, leading to the great war."

Lila had heard stories of the great war, but they were often sanitized versions, taught in history classes. She gestured for Alaric to continue.

"My family," Alaric began, his voice quivering, "was torn apart in that war. My sister, a brilliant technomancer, believed in merging magic and tech. She created devices that were ahead of her time. But one day, one of her experiments went wrong. The magical backlash destroyed our home and took her life."

Lila's eyes widened in sympathy. She had known the faction had deep-seated reasons for their beliefs, but hearing a personal account made it all the more real.

Alaric continued, "I blamed tech for her death. I believed that if she had stuck to pure magic, she would still be alive. That's why I joined the faction. I wanted to prevent such tragedies."

Lila, her voice gentle, said, "I'm so sorry for your loss, Alaric. But times have changed. We've learned from past mistakes. The devices we create now have safety measures. We're more informed, more careful."

Alaric looked at her, his eyes searching, "But can you guarantee that no such accidents will happen again? Can you promise that no more lives will be lost?"

Lila hesitated, then said, "I can't make that promise. Progress always comes with risks. But what I can promise is that we'll do everything in our power to minimize those risks. We'll learn, adapt, and grow. Isn't that what the academy teaches us?"

Alaric smiled sadly, "You remind me so much of my sister. She had the same fire, the same belief. Maybe... maybe it's time for old beliefs to change."

Lila reached out, placing a comforting hand on Alaric's arm, "The past can't be changed, but the future is still unwritten. We can shape it together."

Alaric nodded, "Perhaps it's time for a new chapter. But remember, Lila, with great power comes great responsibility. Always strive for balance."

Lila smiled, "I will. And maybe, just maybe, we can find a way for magic and tech to coexist, not just in devices, but in hearts."

As they exited the alcove, the challenges of the labyrinth awaited. But for Lila, the real challenge was understanding, empathy, and bridging gaps. And in that moment, she had succeeded.

The Faction's Dilemma

The labyrinth's challenges had not only tested the students' skills but also their beliefs. As Lila's team continued to demonstrate the harmonious potential of magic and tech, murmurs of doubt and contemplation spread among the members of the antagonistic faction.

In a dimly lit corner of the arena, several faction members huddled, their expressions a mix of concern and contemplation. Among them was Alaric, who had recently shared his personal story with Lila. Beside him stood Marcellus, a staunch opponent of the integration and a vocal leader within the faction.

"We cannot deny what we've seen," began Alaric, his voice filled with uncertainty. "These students, especially Lila's team, have shown that magic and tech can coexist without the catastrophic results we once feared."

Marcellus scoffed, "It's a ruse, Alaric. A temporary display of harmony. The moment they leave this controlled environment, the dangers will become evident."

A younger member, Selene, chimed in, "But what if they're right? What if we've been holding onto outdated beliefs? I've seen the potential in their devices, the genuine collaboration between magical and technological principles."

Marcellus shot her a sharp look, "You're too young to remember the great war, the devastation it brought. We cannot risk another such catastrophe."

Alaric, his voice firm, countered, "But we also cannot stifle progress, Marcellus. We've seen the benefits firsthand. Lila's goggles, Finn's tech solutions, Elara and Maya's combined knowledge. They've achieved what we once thought impossible."

Marcellus sighed, "Our duty is to protect, Alaric. To ensure history doesn't repeat itself."

"And what if our duty also involves adapting? Changing our perspectives based on new evidence?" Alaric questioned.

The group fell silent, each lost in thought. The weight of their responsibility, the potential for a brighter future, and the shadows of the past weighed heavily on them.

Selene, her voice hesitant, spoke up, "I've been working on a project, a device that uses both magic and tech. I was afraid to share it, given our faction's beliefs. But after witnessing the tournament, I believe it's time."

Marcellus looked at her, surprise evident in his eyes, "You've been dabbling in integration?"

Selene nodded, "And I believe it has the potential to change our world for the better. But I need guidance, support."

Alaric placed a comforting hand on her shoulder, "We must be open to new ideas, Marcellus. Perhaps it's time for our faction to reevaluate our stance."

Marcellus looked torn. The weight of tradition and the potential for innovation battled within him. Finally, he spoke, "We'll consider it. But we proceed with caution. We cannot afford mistakes."

Alaric nodded, "Agreed. But we also cannot afford to be left behind. The world is changing, and we must change with it."

The group dispersed, each member reflecting on the path ahead. The challenges of the labyrinth had not only tested skills but also beliefs. And as the tournament progressed, it became evident that the real challenge lay not in the puzzles and patterns of the arena but in the hearts and minds of its participants.

The Faction's Dilemma had begun as a resistance to change, but as the days unfolded, it transformed into a quest for understanding and growth. The future of the Fairy-Tech Academy, and indeed the world, depended on the choices made in these crucial moments.

Chapter 11: Restoring Balance

The central arena, once a symbol of the Fairy-Tech Academy's grandeur, now bore scars of recent events. The once-pristine floors were marred with scorch marks, and the air still held a lingering tension. But amidst the remnants of chaos, a new energy was taking shape.

Lila, her team, and several others were already at work, their hands and minds busy in restoration. But what was truly remarkable was the sight of members from the antagonistic faction working alongside them. Gone were the days of stark division; the recent events had forged an unexpected alliance.

Elara, with her elemental magic, was mending broken structures, her hands weaving patterns in the air as stone and metal responded to her call. Beside her, a member of the antagonistic faction, a young mage named Orion, was using his earth-based magic to assist. Their combined efforts were a dance of harmony, as magic flowed and intertwined, mending and restoring.

Finn, with his tech gauntlet, was busy recalibrating the arena's systems. He was joined by Selene, a tech prodigy from the opposing faction. Their initial interactions were cautious, but as wires connected and systems rebooted, a mutual respect began to form. They exchanged nods of approval, their previous differences set aside in the face of a common goal.

Maya, her analytical mind always seeking solutions, coordinated the efforts. She was in deep discussion with several members from both factions, their combined knowledge creating a roadmap for restoration. Charts, blueprints, and magical glyphs floated around them, each contributing to the intricate puzzle of restoration.

The arena, which had witnessed competitions, innovations, and even sabotage, was now a testament to collaboration. The very essence of the academy's ethos was on display, as magic and tech, once seen as rivals, now worked in tandem. The combined efforts of the teams symbolized not just the restoration of a physical space but the mending of ideological divides.

As the hours passed, the arena began to regain its former glory. The collaborative spirit was infectious, with more members joining in, offering their skills and expertise. The once-opposing factions were now united, their shared experiences in the arena forging bonds of understanding.

Lila, pausing to survey the progress, felt a swell of pride. The journey had been challenging, filled with trials and tribulations. But the sight before her, of unity and collaboration, was a beacon of hope. The potential harmony between magic and tech was not just a dream; it was a reality taking shape.

Cedric, who had been assisting in the efforts, approached Lila. His expression, once stern and inscrutable, now held a hint of warmth. "It's remarkable," he remarked, his gaze sweeping over the bustling arena. "To see everyone working together, setting aside differences... it's a sight I never imagined."

Lila nodded, her eyes reflecting the same sentiment. "It's a testament to the academy's legacy and the potential of a harmonious future."

The day's efforts culminated in the arena's complete restoration. As the sun set, casting a golden hue over the academy, the central arena stood tall and proud, its scars healed, and its spirit renewed. The combined efforts of the teams, including members of the antagonistic faction, had not only restored a structure but had also paved the way for a new chapter in the academy's history.

Cedric's Change of Heart

The central arena, now restored to its former glory, was alive with the hum of activity. Students, faculty, and guests moved about, discussing the day's events, innovations, and the unexpected challenges. But amidst the crowd, one figure stood still, lost in thought. Cedric, the once staunch opponent of the magic-tech integration, seemed distant, his usual confident demeanor replaced by introspection.

He found a quiet corner, away from the bustling crowd, and sat down, his gaze fixed on a distant point. Memories flooded back, stories of his ancestors who had been pioneers in the realm of magic. They had been revered, their legacy a testament to the power and purity of magic. Growing up, Cedric had been regaled with tales of their exploits, their battles against the encroaching world of technology. It was these stories, these legends, that had shaped his beliefs, his unwavering stance against the integration of magic and tech.

But today, he had witnessed something that challenged those beliefs. The collaborative spirit, the unity of purpose, and the undeniable benefits of combining magic and technology were evident. Lila's team, with their innovative solutions and their ability to rise above challenges, had showcased the potential of a harmonious coexistence.

Cedric recalled a particular story, one that his grandfather had often narrated. It was about a great mage who had faced a similar dilemma when the first signs of technology had emerged. The mage, torn between tradition and progress, had chosen to isolate himself, believing that magic in its purest form was the only way forward. But in his isolation, he had missed out on the evolution of the world, the potential of combining the old with the new.

A soft voice interrupted his thoughts. "Deep in reflection, I see." It was Professor Eldrin, his wise eyes observing Cedric with a knowing look.

Cedric looked up, a hint of vulnerability in his eyes. "I've always believed in the purity of magic, Professor. But today, I've seen the potential of what can be achieved when we embrace change."

Professor Eldrin nodded, taking a seat beside Cedric. "Change is inevitable, Cedric. But it's how we respond to it that defines us. Your ancestors were great mages, but they lived in a different time. The world is evolving, and we must evolve with it."

Cedric sighed, "I've been so blinded by my family's legacy that I failed to see the bigger picture. The potential of a world where magic and tech coexist, where they complement and elevate each other."

The Professor smiled, "It's never too late to change, Cedric. The academy has always been a place of learning, not just of magic and tech, but of life's lessons. Today, you've learned one such lesson."

Cedric nodded, a newfound determination in his eyes. "I want to be a part of this change, Professor. I want to contribute, to learn, and to help shape a future where magic and tech thrive together."

Professor Eldrin patted Cedric's back, "That's the spirit. Remember, it's not about forgetting our past, but about building on it, creating a future that honors our legacy while embracing the possibilities of tomorrow."

As the two continued their conversation, the central arena, with its blend of magic and technology, stood as a testament to the academy's ethos. Cedric, once a staunch opponent, was now on the cusp of a transformation, ready to embrace a world of boundless possibilities.

The Essence of Magic-Tech Synergy

As the sun began its descent, casting a golden hue over the academy grounds, a hush fell over the central arena. Students, faculty, and guests gathered in anticipation. They were about to witness a demonstration that would delve into the very heart of the academy's ethos: the synergy between magic and technology.

Professor Eldrin, a tall, imposing figure with a silver mane and piercing blue eyes, took center stage. Beside him stood a group of senior students, each representing a unique blend of magical and technological expertise. The air was thick with excitement.

"Today," began Professor Eldrin, his voice echoing through the arena, "we stand at the crossroads of tradition and innovation. We have seen the power of collaboration, the potential of combining our magical heritage with the advancements of technology. But how does this synergy truly work?"

One of the senior students, Elaran, stepped forward, holding a small crystal orb. "Magic," she began, "is the essence of our world. It flows through everything, from the air we breathe to the ground we walk on." She channeled her energy into the orb, which began to glow with a soft, ethereal light. "But by itself, magic is raw, untamed."

Another student, Orion, with a mechanical arm that was a marvel of engineering, continued, "Technology, on the other hand, is the result of human ingenuity. It's precise, calculated." He connected his arm to the orb, and intricate patterns of light began to dance across its surface. "But it lacks the soul, the essence that magic provides."

Professor Eldrin nodded, "The arena's design embodies this principle. It's not just bricks and mortar. It's a living, breathing entity, where magic and tech coexist, enhancing each other."

A third student, Lyria, known for her expertise in elemental magic, conjured a small whirlwind. Simultaneously, a series of drones, controlled by tech prodigy, Jaxon, flew into the whirlwind, stabilizing it. Together, they created a mesmerizing dance of wind and light.

"The principles behind this integration are based on balance," Professor Eldrin explained. "Magic provides the energy, the life force. Technology offers control, direction. When combined, they create something greater than the sum of their parts."

The demonstration continued, with students showcasing various magic-tech integrations. There was a water spell combined with a filtration system, turning polluted water pure. A fire spell was harnessed to power a steam engine, demonstrating efficient energy conversion.

As the demonstrations concluded, Professor Eldrin addressed the gathering once more. "The potential of magic-tech synergy is limitless.

But it requires understanding, respect, and collaboration. We must move beyond our biases, our preconceived notions, and embrace the future with an open heart."

The crowd erupted in applause, the energy palpable. They had witnessed not just a demonstration of skills but a vision of the future, a promise of a world where magic and technology coexisted in harmony.

As the evening shadows lengthened, the arena once again became a hub of activity, with students discussing the demonstrations, sharing ideas, and dreaming of innovations. The essence of magic-tech synergy had been unveiled, and it held the promise of a brighter, more integrated future.

Reflections and Resolutions

The evening sky painted a canvas of deep purples and golds, casting a serene ambiance over the academy grounds. Students, both old allies and new, gathered in small clusters, their conversations a blend of excitement, introspection, and newfound understanding.

Lila, her hair catching the last rays of the sun, sat with a diverse group of students. Among them were members of the antagonistic faction, their previous animosities now replaced with mutual respect. "Today," she began, her voice soft yet firm, "we've seen the power of unity, the strength that comes from setting aside our differences and working towards a common goal."

A young mage from the faction, Alaric, nodded. "I never imagined I'd be working alongside tech enthusiasts," he admitted, "but seeing the potential of magic-tech integration, witnessing its wonders... it's opened my eyes."

Beside him, Tessa, a tech prodigy, smiled. "It's easy to get caught up in our beliefs, to see the world through a narrow lens. But today, we've broadened our horizons. We've seen that magic and tech, when combined, can achieve wonders."

The conversations around them echoed similar sentiments. Students shared their experiences, the challenges they faced, the moments of doubt, and the triumphs. They spoke of the importance of understanding, of listening, of learning from one another.

In a quiet corner, Cedric sat deep in thought. The weight of his family's legacy, the pressure of their expectations, had always been a burden. But today, he'd seen a different path, one of collaboration and coexistence. He'd witnessed the power of unity, the potential of combining the old with the new. And it had changed him.

"I've been so blinded by my beliefs," he confessed to a group of students, "so caught up in the past that I failed to see the present, the possibilities of the future." He paused, taking a deep breath. "But today, I've seen the power of collaboration, the strength that comes from understanding and unity. And it's given me hope."

As the evening deepened, Professor Eldrin addressed the gathering. "Today," he began, "we've taken a significant step towards a harmonious coexistence. We've seen the potential of magic-tech synergy, the wonders it can achieve. But this is just the beginning. The journey ahead is long, filled with challenges and obstacles. But if we stand together, if we learn from one another, there's no limit to what we can achieve."

The students listened, rapt, hanging on to every word. They'd experienced the power of unity, the strength that came from setting aside differences and working towards a common goal. And they were determined to carry that spirit forward, to build a world where magic and tech coexisted in harmony.

As the night deepened, the central arena, now stable and restored, stood as a testament to their efforts, a symbol of hope and unity. The students, their hearts filled with newfound understanding and resolve, left the arena, their steps echoing with determination.

Chapter 12: Revelations and Reconciliation

The grand hall of the academy was awash with a golden hue, the result of countless enchanted lanterns floating above. The vast space, usually echoing with the cacophony of student debates and laughter, was now filled with an air of solemnity and anticipation. Rows of seats were filled to capacity, with students, faculty, and special guests in attendance. The walls, usually adorned with portraits of past luminaries, now bore banners celebrating the post-tournament achievements.

At the front of the hall, a raised platform was set, where the academy's elders sat in their ceremonial robes. Their presence, always commanding respect, felt even more significant today. The eldest among them, Elder Miriam, rose to address the gathering.

"Today," she began, her voice resonating with warmth, "we gather not just to celebrate the end of a tournament, but to honor the spirit of innovation, collaboration, and unity that it represented."

A hush fell over the crowd as she continued, "Every participant showed commendable skill and determination. But there was one team that truly embodied the essence of what we aim to achieve here at the academy."

All eyes turned to Lila and her team, seated together, their hands intertwined in mutual support. "Lila's team," Elder Miriam announced, "has shown us the future. Their innovative approach to merging magic and tech was not just impressive but inspirational."

The hall erupted in applause, the sound echoing like a powerful spell. Lila's eyes glistened with tears of pride, while Finn, Elara, and Maya beamed, their faces reflecting the joy of recognition. They had faced skepticism, challenges, and even sabotage, but this moment made it all worth it.

Elder Miriam gestured for them to rise. "Please, come forward."

As they approached the platform, the applause grew louder, a testament to their achievement. Lila felt a rush of emotions. The weight of their accomplishment, the pride in their innovation, and the hope for a future where magic and tech coexisted harmoniously.

Elder Miriam handed them a crystalline trophy, its facets reflecting the golden light of the hall. "This is not just a trophy," she whispered so only they could hear, "but a symbol of a new dawn for our academy and the world beyond."

Lila held the trophy high, and the hall once again erupted in cheers. The other teams, including some from the antagonistic faction, acknowledged them with nods and claps, a sign of respect and perhaps a hint of changed perspectives.

As they returned to their seats, Lila felt a hand on her shoulder. Turning, she found herself face to face with a member of the antagonistic faction. "Well done," he said, his voice sincere. It was a small gesture, but it spoke volumes.

The ceremony continued, but for Lila and her team, this moment of recognition, amidst the grandeur of the academy's grand hall, would forever be etched in their memories. They had not just won a tournament; they had ignited a beacon of hope for a harmonious future.

The applause for Lila's team had barely subsided when Elder Nathaniel, a figure of immense respect and wisdom, rose from his seat. The room, still buzzing with the energy of the previous accolades, grew silent. Elder Nathaniel's presence always commanded attention, but today, there was a gravity in his demeanor that was palpable.

"Today, we celebrate the achievements of our young ones," he began, his voice deep and resonant. "But to truly understand the significance of their accomplishments, we must remember our past."

He paused, taking a moment to gather his thoughts. "Many of you are aware of the faction's existence, but few know the true story of its formation. It is a tale of tragedy, resilience, and hope."

The audience leaned forward, captivated. Even those who had heard whispers of the faction's history were eager to hear it from Elder Nathaniel.

"Centuries ago," he continued, "our world was not divided by magic and tech. They coexisted, complementing each other. But a catastrophic event changed everything."

His eyes, usually bright with wisdom, darkened with sorrow. "A great explosion, the result of an experiment gone wrong, tore through our land. It decimated cities, destroyed families, and left a scar on our world that can still be felt today."

Murmurs of shock and sadness rippled through the hall. Many had heard of the explosion, but the magnitude of its impact was becoming clear.

"The aftermath was devastating. The balance between magic and tech was shattered. Blame was cast, with each side accusing the other of causing the disaster. Trust was broken, and our world was divided."

Elder Nathaniel's voice grew softer, more personal. "Many families were affected, including one that is very dear to our academy. Cedric's ancestors."

A collective gasp filled the room. All eyes turned to Cedric, who sat rigidly, his face pale but composed.

"They were pioneers, visionaries who believed in the harmony of magic and tech. But they paid a heavy price. They lost their homes, their loved ones, and were ostracized for their beliefs."

Elder Nathaniel's gaze met Cedric's. "But they did not give up. They formed the faction, a group dedicated to restoring the balance between magic and tech. They faced ridicule, opposition, and even threats, but their conviction never wavered."

The room was silent, the weight of the revelation sinking in. The faction, often misunderstood and maligned, had its roots in a noble cause.

Elder Nathaniel continued, "It is essential to remember our history, not to dwell on the pain, but to learn from it. To understand the sacrifices made by those before us and to strive for a better future."

He looked around the room, his gaze sweeping over the students, the faculty, and the guests. "Today, we see a glimmer of that future. Lila's team has shown us the potential of merging magic and tech. But let us not forget the path that led us here."

He paused, letting his words sink in. "Let us honor the brave souls who came before us, who faced adversity with courage and determination. Let us remember the faction's true purpose and work towards a world where magic and tech coexist in harmony."

As Elder Nathaniel took his seat, the room erupted in applause, not just for Lila's team but for the faction's legacy and the hope of a united future.

Cedric, usually stoic and reserved, was visibly moved. The weight of his family's history, the pain of their sacrifices, and the hope for a better future all converged in this moment. The next part of the ceremony would be his chance to share his personal connection to the tragic event and its influence on his beliefs. But for now, he took a deep breath, preparing himself for what was to come.

Cedric's Openness

The grand hall was still echoing with the remnants of Elder Nathaniel's revelations when Cedric slowly rose from his seat. The room, which moments ago was filled with applause and murmurs, fell into a hushed silence. Every eye was on him, the weight of his family's legacy palpable in the air.

Cedric took a deep breath, his usually confident demeanor replaced by a vulnerability that few had seen. "I never thought I'd share this story," he began, his voice trembling slightly. "But after hearing Elder Nathaniel's words, I believe it's time."

He paused, gathering his thoughts. "The tragic event that led to the formation of the faction is not just a historical account for me. It's personal. It's my family's story."

A murmur of sympathy rippled through the audience. Many had known of Cedric's connection to the faction, but few knew the depth of his ties.

"My ancestors were visionaries," Cedric continued. "They believed in the harmonious coexistence of magic and tech. But their dreams were shattered that fateful day. The explosion took away their homes, their loved ones, and their dreams."

His voice cracked with emotion. "My great-grandfather was just a child when it happened. He lost his parents, his siblings, and was left to fend for himself in a world that blamed him for the very tragedy that had orphaned him."

The audience was rapt, hanging on to every word. The pain and loss that Cedric's family had endured were palpable.

"But he didn't let the tragedy define him," Cedric said, his voice gaining strength. "He channeled his pain into purpose. He became one of the founding members of the faction, dedicating his life to restoring the balance between magic and tech."

Cedric paused, taking a moment to collect himself. "Growing up, I heard stories of the sacrifices my ancestors made. The ridicule they faced, the threats they endured. But they never wavered in their conviction."

He looked around the room, his gaze meeting Lila's. "Their legacy is the reason I'm here today. It's the reason I've dedicated my life to the academy and the harmonious integration of magic and tech."

A tear rolled down Cedric's cheek, but he made no move to wipe it away. "I've always believed that understanding our past is crucial to shaping our future. My family's story is a testament to the resilience of the human spirit, the power of conviction, and the importance of unity."

He took a deep breath, his voice filled with determination. "I stand before you today, not just as a member of the academy, but as a descendant of the faction. I carry their legacy, their dreams, and their hopes. And I vow to do everything in my power to ensure that their sacrifices were not in vain."

The room was silent, the weight of Cedric's words sinking in. The pain, the loss, and the hope of his family's story had touched everyone.

Lila, who had always admired Cedric for his strength and leadership, felt a newfound respect for him. She realized that behind his stoic exterior was a man with deep convictions, shaped by a legacy of pain and resilience.

Elder Nathaniel, who had known Cedric since he was a child, was visibly moved. He rose from his seat and approached Cedric, placing a comforting hand on his shoulder. "Your ancestors would be proud," he whispered, his voice filled with emotion.

Cedric nodded, tears streaming down his face. "Thank you, Elder Nathaniel," he replied, his voice choked with emotion. "I hope to honor their legacy and make a difference in this world."

As Cedric took his seat, the room erupted in applause. The students, faculty, and guests were all moved by his heartfelt revelation. It was a moment of deep introspection, a reminder of the importance of understanding our past and the power of conviction.

The ceremony continued, but the atmosphere had shifted. There was a newfound sense of unity and purpose, a collective determination to work towards a better future. And as Lila and her team prepared for their magic-tech demonstration, they knew they had the support and admiration of the entire academy.

Mysterious Observer

Tucked away in a dimly lit corner, a figure stood, draped in a cloak of deep midnight blue. The fabric seemed to absorb the light around it, making the figure appear as a silhouette against the opulence of the hall. The only discernible feature was an emblem embroidered on the cloak—a serpent intertwined with a circuit board, its eyes gleaming with a ruby red hue.

The figure's gaze was unwavering, fixed intently on Lila and Maya. Every so often, the figure would pull out a small, ornate device, making notes or perhaps recording observations. The device emitted a faint glow, illuminating a face obscured by a hood. Sharp, angular features, and eyes that glittered with an inscrutable intent.

As the evening progressed, whispers began to circulate among the attendees. "Who is that?" one student murmured to another, nodding subtly towards the mysterious observer.

"I've never seen him before," the other replied, eyes wide with curiosity. "But that emblem... it's familiar. I've seen it in the forbidden archives."

Another elder, catching wind of the whispers, approached the figure with a cautious stride. "Greetings," he began, his voice firm yet polite. "It's not often we have observers at our ceremonies. May I inquire as to your affiliation?"

The figure paused, the ambient noise of the hall seeming to fade into the background. Slowly, they lifted their head, revealing a pair of piercing eyes that seemed to see right through the elder. "I am but a humble scholar," came the reply, the voice smooth and measured. "I have a keen interest in the fusion of magic and technology. Your academy's advancements are... notable."

The elder, taken aback by the figure's intense demeanor, nodded slowly. "Well, you are welcome here. But might I ask about your emblem? It's quite unique."

The figure's fingers brushed over the embroidered serpent, a hint of a smile playing on their lips. "It's a symbol of my order. We believe in the balance of magic and tech, much like your academy. But our methods... differ."

Before the elder could press further, the figure slipped away, melting into the shadows of the hall. The elder was left standing, a chill running down his spine. He had been around for centuries, and very few things unsettled him. But this mysterious observer, with their cryptic emblem and enigmatic demeanor, had managed to do just that.

The ceremony continued, but the presence of the observer left an undercurrent of unease. Students and elders alike cast furtive glances towards the corner where the figure had stood, but there was no trace of them.

As the evening drew to a close, and the attendees began to depart, the whispers continued. Who was this mysterious observer? What was their intent? And what did their emblem signify?

The questions hung in the air, unanswered. But one thing was certain—the academy's journey into the fusion of magic and tech had attracted attention, and not all of it was benign. The path ahead was fraught with challenges and intrigue, and the mysterious observer was just the beginning.

Chapter 13: New Alliances and Future Endeavors

The academy's vast corridors and open courtyards buzzed with a renewed sense of purpose. Everywhere one looked, clusters of students huddled together, animatedly discussing their ideas, sketching out plans, and setting up experimental stations. The merger of magic and tech had ignited a spark, and the students were eager to fan its flames.

Lila, having inspired many with her team's demonstration, was at the forefront of a project that aimed to create a device that could harness ambient magical energy and convert it into a usable power source. Her team had set up a makeshift lab in one of the academy's sunlit atriums, where a series of crystalline structures stood, glowing faintly as they absorbed the magical aura of the surroundings.

A few corridors down, a group of tech enthusiasts led by a third-year student named Jasper were working on integrating spell runes into circuit boards. Their goal was to create a computer that could be powered and operated using both electricity and magic. The room was filled with the hum of machinery and the soft glow of runes, creating a mesmerizing dance of light and shadow.

In the academy's gardens, a botanical project was underway. Helmed by a duo, Clara and Theo, they were attempting to infuse plants with tech sensors, allowing them to communicate their needs—water, sunlight, nutrients—directly to a connected app. The garden was a riot of colors, with plants glowing in neon shades, signaling their requirements.

The spirit of collaboration was palpable. Students from different years and specializations came together, pooling their knowledge and resources. It was not uncommon to see a senior mage instructing a freshman on the nuances of a particular spell, or a tech whiz explaining the intricacies of a circuit to a magic enthusiast.

Amidst all this, the academy's library became a hub of activity. Students poured over ancient tomes and modern tech manuals, seeking knowledge that could aid their projects. Librarians, usually sticklers for silence, seemed to have relaxed their rules, allowing the library to be filled with the soft murmur of discussions and the occasional cheer of a breakthrough.

One particularly ambitious project was set up in the academy's central courtyard. A massive holographic display, powered by both tech and magic, showcased the various projects in real-time. Students could interact with the display, gather information, and even offer their expertise to projects that piqued their interest.

As days turned into nights and nights into days, the academy was transformed. Sleep became a luxury as students worked tirelessly, fueled by passion and the thrill of innovation. The boundaries between magic and tech began to blur, and in their place arose a new paradigm, one that promised endless possibilities.

The collaborative projects were not just about innovation; they were a testament to the academy's spirit. A spirit that believed in pushing boundaries, challenging norms, and above all, the power of unity. For in the union of magic and tech, the students of the academy had discovered a truth - that together, they could create a world beyond imagination.

Finn's Tech Workshop

The sun cast a warm, golden hue over the academy's central courtyard, where a large white tent had been erected. A sign at the entrance read, "Finn's Tech Workshop," and students of all ages eagerly queued up, their faces filled with anticipation.

Inside the tent, tables were laden with an array of gadgets, tools, and devices. There were drones hovering in mid-air, holographic displays showcasing intricate 3D models, and robotic arms deftly assembling miniature structures. The air was thick with the scent of soldering and the hum of machinery.

At the center of it all was Finn, a tall, lanky figure with tousled brown hair and glasses that perpetually slid down his nose. He moved from one table to the next, explaining the workings of a particular device or demonstrating a new piece of tech. His enthusiasm was infectious, and students hung on to his every word.

As the workshop progressed, Finn climbed onto a makeshift stage at the far end of the tent. He cleared his throat, and the chatter died down. "I want to share a story with you all," he began, his voice tinged with emotion. "A story that shaped my love for technology."

He spoke of a rainy evening from his childhood when he had stumbled upon an old, discarded radio in his attic. With childlike curiosity, he had taken it apart, marveling at the intricate circuits and wires. That evening, with the help of a manual and sheer determination, young Finn had managed to bring the radio back to life.

"The joy I felt when I heard that first crackle of sound, the music that flowed from that old radio, was indescribable," Finn reminisced. "It was a defining moment for me. I realized the power of technology, the magic it held. From that day on, I was hooked."

The students listened, rapt, as Finn recounted late nights spent tinkering with gadgets, the countless failures, and the triumphant successes. He spoke of his journey, from a curious child to a student at the academy, and now, as a mentor, eager to share his knowledge.

The workshop wasn't just about showcasing tech; it was a testament to Finn's passion. He wanted students to see beyond the circuits and codes, to understand the stories, the emotions, and the dreams that technology held within.

As the sun began to set, casting long shadows across the courtyard, students gathered around Finn, seeking advice, sharing their projects, or simply thanking him for the inspiration. The atmosphere was electric, charged with ideas and possibilities.

Finn's workshop was more than just a display of gadgets; it was a celebration of innovation, creativity, and the indomitable human spirit. It reminded everyone present that technology wasn't just about machines and codes; it was about the stories they told, the dreams they realized, and the future they promised.

And as the last of the students left the tent, Finn stood there, looking at the empty tables, the discarded tools, and the lingering traces of magic in the air. A smile played on his lips, for he knew that he had ignited a spark, a spark that would light up the world of magic and tech for generations to come.

Elara's Magical Seminar

The sun had barely begun its descent when students and faculty alike started to gather in the academy's largest lecture hall. Whispers of excitement filled the air, punctuated by the occasional gasp as attendees caught sight of the room's transformation. The usually austere hall was now bathed in a soft, ethereal glow, with shimmering symbols floating in the air and delicate, luminescent flowers sprouting from the walls.

At the front stood Elara, her raven-black hair cascading down her back, contrasting starkly with her pale blue robes. Her eyes, usually sharp and piercing, held a softness today, a reflection of the passion she was about to share.

As the last of the attendees settled down, a hush fell over the room. Elara raised her hands, and the symbols in the air began to dance, weaving intricate patterns as she began to speak.

"Magic," she began, her voice echoing softly, "is the very essence of our world. It is the heartbeat that courses through our veins, the breath that gives life to our dreams." She paused, letting the weight of her words sink in. "Today, I will take you on a journey, a deep dive into the world of spells, rituals, and the very fabric of magic itself."

The next hour was a mesmerizing display of magical prowess. Elara conjured illusions that danced across the room, summoned creatures from ancient tales, and demonstrated spells that left even the most seasoned mages in awe. But more than the displays of power, it was the stories she wove, the history and lore of magic, that captivated her audience.

Yet, amidst the sea of enchanted faces, a few stood out. Members of the antagonistic faction, their expressions a mix of skepticism and grudging respect. Their presence was a stark reminder of the rift that existed, the differing beliefs that had caused so much strife.

Elara, ever the diplomat, acknowledged them with a nod. "I see we have some guests today," she said, her voice neutral. "While our beliefs may differ, our love for magic is the same. I invite you to join us, to share in the wonder and beauty of the arcane."

The seminar continued, with students and faction members alike participating in discussions, sharing their perspectives, and even demonstrating their own spells. It was a rare moment of unity, a glimpse into a world where magic was a bridge, not a barrier.

As the seminar drew to a close, Elara addressed the room once more. "Magic is not just spells and rituals," she said, her voice filled with emotion. "It is a legacy, a gift passed down through generations. It is our duty to cherish it, to use it wisely, and to ensure its survival for the generations to come."

The applause that followed was deafening, a testament to the impact of her words. Students and faculty left the hall with a renewed sense of purpose, their hearts filled with hope and determination.

But as the room emptied, Elara's gaze lingered on the members of the antagonistic faction. Their expressions were inscrutable, but she could sense the shift, the tiny cracks in their resolve. The seminar had been a success, not just in sharing knowledge, but in building bridges and encouraging understanding.

And as she left the hall, Elara couldn't help but hope that this was just the beginning, a small step towards a future where magic was celebrated, not feared.

Mysterious Encounter

The seminar had reached its zenith, with students and faculty deeply engrossed in Elara's magical demonstrations. The room was a symphony of gasps, applause, and whispered conversations. But amidst the crowd, Maya, a young mage with a penchant for tech, felt a cold draft brush past her. It was subtle, almost imperceptible, but enough to make her turn.

Standing at the edge of the room, partially concealed by the shadows, was the mysterious figure. Dressed in a dark cloak, their face was obscured, save for a pair of piercing eyes that seemed to glow with an otherworldly light. Those eyes were fixed on Maya.

Feeling a magnetic pull, Maya found herself walking towards the figure. As she approached, the mysterious individual stepped forward, revealing an emblem embroidered on their cloak—a balance scale, with one side representing magic and the other, technology.

"You are Maya, are you not?" The voice was soft, almost melodic, but carried an undertone of authority.

Taken aback, Maya nodded. "Yes, I am. Who are you?"

The figure tilted their head slightly, considering her. "A seeker of truths, much like yourself. Tell me, young mage, what do you believe is the true balance between magic and tech?"

Maya hesitated. The question was one she had pondered often, especially given the academy's recent endeavors. "I believe they can coexist, complementing each other. Magic gives us the power to dream, while tech allows us to realize those dreams."

The mysterious figure seemed to consider her answer, their eyes narrowing slightly. "An interesting perspective. But what if one were to overpower the other? What if the balance tipped?"

Maya frowned, sensing the depth of the question. "Then it would be our responsibility to restore it. Both magic and tech have their strengths and weaknesses. It's up to us to ensure they work in harmony."

A soft chuckle escaped the figure. "Wise words, young mage. Remember them well." And with that, they began to retreat into the shadows.

"Wait!" Maya called out, taking a step forward. "Who are you? Why did you ask me that question?"

The figure paused, their silhouette barely visible against the dim light. "All in due time, Maya. For now, continue seeking, continue questioning. The answers you seek may be closer than you think."

And just like that, they vanished, leaving Maya standing alone, her heart racing. The weight of the encounter pressed down on her, filling her with a mix of curiosity and unease.

As the seminar concluded and the attendees began to disperse, Maya's thoughts were consumed by the mysterious figure and their cryptic question. Who were they? What did they want? And why had they singled her out?

She shared the encounter with a few close friends, who were equally intrigued. Some speculated that the figure might be a member of a secret society, while others believed they were a messenger from another realm.

But as the days turned into weeks, the encounter faded into the background, overshadowed by the academy's ongoing projects and events. Yet, the figure's words remained etched in Maya's mind, a constant reminder of the delicate balance between magic and tech, and the responsibility that came with it.

Unbeknownst to Maya, the mysterious figure continued to watch from the shadows, their interest in the young mage far from over. The balance they spoke of was more than just a philosophical question—it was a prophecy, one that Maya would soon find herself at the center of.

Chapter 14: A New Horizon

The academy's main courtyard was bustling with activity. Students were preparing for the closing ceremony, arranging chairs and setting up magical displays. Amidst the chaos, Lila found herself drawn to a secluded corner where an ancient oak tree stood. Its branches stretched out, providing shade and a sense of serenity.

As Lila approached, she noticed an elder sitting beneath the tree. The elder's eyes were closed, and she seemed to be in deep meditation. Lila recognized her as Elder Mirana, one of the most respected figures in the magical community. She had heard stories about her wisdom and her ability to see beyond the present.

Elder Mirana opened her eyes, her gaze meeting Lila's. "Ah, Lila," she said with a gentle smile. "I've been waiting for you."

Lila was taken aback. "For me? Why?"

Elder Mirana beckoned her closer. "There's something I need to give you" she said, reaching into her robe and producing a small, intricately designed box.

Lila took the box, her fingers brushing against the cold metal. As she opened it, her breath caught in her throat. Inside lay a pendant, its surface adorned with symbols that shimmered and danced in the sunlight. At its center was an emblem, one that Lila had seen before—on the mysterious figure.

"This artifact," Elder Mirana began, "has been in our academy for centuries. It is said to hold the power to bridge the worlds of magic and technology. And now, it is yours."

Lila looked up, confusion evident in her eyes. "Why me? "

Elder Mirana smiled. "You have shown great potential, Lila. This artifact chooses its bearer, and it has chosen you. It is a legacy, a responsibility, and a guide for the adventures that lie ahead. This is the real mystery prize"

Lila held the pendant, feeling its weight and the energy it radiated. The symbols seemed to come alive, whispering secrets of the past and hinting at future challenges.

Elder Mirana continued, "The emblem at its center is a symbol of unity, a reminder that magic and technology can coexist harmoniously. But it also suggests a connection to the mysterious figure you've encountered. You must discover the link and unlock the true potential of this artifact."

Lila nodded, determination burning in her eyes. "I will, Elder Mirana. I promise."

Elder Mirana placed a hand on Lila's shoulder. "Remember, Lila, with great power comes great responsibility. Cherish this artifact, protect it, and let it guide you on your journey."

As Lila left the courtyard, the pendant around her neck, she felt a mix of excitement and apprehension. The weight of the legacy she now carried was immense, but she was ready to embrace it and uncover the mysteries it held. The artifact was not just a gift; it was a challenge, a call to adventure, and Lila was determined to rise to the occasion.

Foreshadowing Sequel

The sun was beginning its descent, casting a golden hue over the academy's main courtyard. Students were engaged in animated discussions, their voices filled with excitement and anticipation for the closing ceremony. Lila, however, found herself distracted. The weight of the artifact around her neck served as a constant reminder of the legacy she now carried.

She decided to take a moment to herself, moving towards a quiet alcove near the edge of the courtyard. As she held the artifact in her hand, examining its intricate design, she felt a strange sensation, as if being watched. She looked around, trying to shake off the feeling, but her gaze was drawn to a distant balcony.

There, shrouded in shadows, stood the mysterious figure. The emblem on their cloak matched the one on Lila's artifact, confirming their connection. Their eyes locked for a brief moment, and Lila could sense a mix of curiosity and caution emanating from the figure.

Suddenly, a gust of wind blew through the courtyard, and when Lila looked up again, the figure had vanished. But the brief encounter left her with more questions than answers. Who was this enigmatic individual? What was their connection to the artifact? And why were they observing her?

Lila's thoughts were interrupted by Cedric, who approached her with a concerned expression. "Lila, are you alright? You seem...distracted."

She hesitated for a moment, debating whether to share her encounter with him. "I saw the mysterious figure again," she finally admitted. "They were watching me from a distance, especially when I was holding the artifact."

Cedric's eyes widened in surprise. "That's...unsettling. But it also confirms that there's a deeper connection between you, the artifact, and that figure. We need to be cautious."

Lila nodded in agreement. "I know. But I also feel like this is just the beginning. There's so much we don't know, and I have a feeling that this artifact will lead us to more adventures."

Cedric smiled, placing a reassuring hand on her shoulder. "Whatever lies ahead, we'll face it together. But for now, let's focus on the closing ceremony."

As they rejoined the festivities, Lila couldn't shake off the feeling of anticipation. The mysterious figure's presence hinted at challenges and adventures that lay ahead. The artifact was not just a legacy; it was a key to unlocking new mysteries and forging new alliances.

The courtyard was bathed in the soft glow of the twilight, a gentle breeze whispering through the ancient trees that stood as silent witnesses to the academy's rich history. Students, faculty, and distinguished guests gathered in a semi-circle, their faces reflecting the golden hues of the setting sun. The headmistress, a figure of wisdom and guidance, stepped forward to address the assembly, her presence commanding a respectful silence.

"Today marks the culmination of a journey, a testament to the resilience and unity that has blossomed within these hallowed walls," he began, his voice echoing through the courtyard. "We have witnessed the merging of worlds, the harmonious blend of magic and technology, forging a path towards a brighter tomorrow."

He paused, allowing his words to resonate with the audience. Lila stood among her peers, the weight of the artifact around her neck a tangible reminder of the responsibilities and adventures that awaited her.

"As we stand on the cusp of a new era, let us remember the lessons we have learned," the Headmistress continued. "The importance of understanding and empathy, the value of collaboration, and the boundless potential that lies within each one of us."

The crowd listened intently, absorbing the gravity of his words. The Headmistress's eyes met Lila's, and she could feel the depth of his wisdom and the hope he harboured for the future.

"We have seen the transformation of individuals, the forging of unlikely alliances, and the birth of innovative ideas," he said, his gaze sweeping across the faces of the young students who represented the future. "You are the pioneers of a new age, the bearers of a legacy that transcends the boundaries of magic and technology."

As he spoke, the courtyard seemed to come alive, the ancient stones resonating with the energy of the words being spoken. The trees swayed gently, as if in agreement, their leaves rustling in a symphony of unity and hope.

"But let us not forget the challenges that lie ahead," the Headmistress cautioned, his tone shifting to one of solemnity. "The road to harmony is fraught with obstacles, and it is our duty to navigate them with wisdom and courage."

He raised his hands, and a hushed silence fell upon the crowd. "As we close this chapter, let us carry forth the spirit of unity, the desire for understanding, and the pursuit of a brighter tomorrow."

With that, he stepped back, and a chorus of voices rose in unison, singing an ancient hymn that spoke of hope, unity, and the promise of a new dawn. The melody soared into the twilight sky, intertwining with the golden rays of the setting sun, creating a blend of sound and light that seemed to encapsulate the essence of the academy's vision.

Lila felt a surge of emotion, a mixture of pride, anticipation, and a hint of sadness as she realized that this chapter of her life was coming to a close. But as she looked around at the faces of her friends, her mentors, and the community that had become her family, she knew that this was not an end, but a beginning.

A beginning of a journey that would see them forge new paths, explore unknown territories, and perhaps, just perhaps, usher in an era of harmony and prosperity.

As the hymn reached its crescendo, the crowd erupted into applause, their cheers echoing through the courtyard, a testament to the unity and hope that had become the cornerstone of the academy's philosophy.

And as the sun dipped below the horizon, the courtyard was bathed in a gentle glow, a beacon of light in a world on the brink of a new and promising dawn.

Homecoming Celebration

The journey from the academy to Lila's home was a short one, but it felt like an eternity. The weight of the ancient artifact, the memories of the past weeks, and the anticipation of seeing her family again made every step feel heavy yet purposeful.

As she approached her family's residence, the familiar scent of blooming jasmine and the distant sound of laughter reached her ears. The house, a quaint structure with ivy-covered walls and a red-tiled roof, stood as a symbol of warmth, love, and memories. The front yard was alive with activity. Tables were set, lanterns hung from the trees, and the air was filled with the tantalizing aroma of freshly cooked food.

Lila's younger siblings, Mia and Theo, were the first to spot her. They raced towards her, their faces lit up with joy. "Lila!" Mia squealed, throwing her arms around her sister. Theo, trying to act more mature than his ten years, gave Lila a firm handshake, but his twinkling eyes betrayed his excitement.

Their parents soon joined the reunion, their faces a mix of relief and pride. "Look at you," her mother whispered, brushing a stray lock of hair from Lila's face. "Our little mage-tech expert."

Lila chuckled, "I've learned a lot, but there's still so much more to explore."

The evening progressed with stories, laughter, and music. Lila recounted her adventures at the academy, the challenges they faced, and the friendships she forged. She spoke of the mysterious artifact and the emblem that hinted at a legacy far greater than she could fathom. Her family listened intently, their faces reflecting a mix of awe, concern, and pride.

As the night deepened, Lila and her father sat on the porch, gazing at the stars. "The academy has changed, hasn't it?" he mused.

Lila nodded, "It's evolving, just like the world around us. Magic and technology are no longer at odds. They're merging, creating something new, something... beautiful."

Her father smiled, "And you're at the forefront of it all. But remember, with great power comes great responsibility."

Lila looked at the artifact, its surface shimmering in the moonlight. "I know, Dad. This artifact, it's not just a piece of history. It's a responsibility, a legacy."

He squeezed her hand, "And I have no doubt you'll honor it."

The night wore on, and as the lanterns dimmed, Lila felt a profound sense of contentment. The academy had given her knowledge, purpose, and friends. But home, with its familiar sounds, scents, and faces, gave her something equally precious - a sense of belonging.

She went to bed that night with a heart full of gratitude, the artifact safely tucked away. The future was uncertain, filled with challenges and adventures. But for now, in the embrace of her family and the comfort of her home, Lila felt ready to face whatever lay ahead

Don't miss out!

Visit the website below and you can sign up to receive emails whenever Z Thornton publishes a new book. There's no charge and no obligation.

https://books2read.com/r/B-A-ZKYEB-QCMZC

BOOKS 2 READ

Connecting independent readers to independent writers.

About the Author

Hailing from the vibrant landscapes of South Africa, Zayd Thornton is a fresh voice in the realm of fantasy literature, embarking on their inaugural journey as an aspiring author. As a child, the magic of stories captivated their heart, leading them through countless adventures within the pages of books. This early passion for tales of wonder never waned but instead blossomed into a desire to craft their own enchanting narratives.

While their tales might not directly draw from South African lore, the spirit of the country – its vibrancy, resilience, and creativity – subtly influences every page of this debut work. "Fairy-Tech Academy: Magic Meets Machinery" stands as a testament to Zayd Thornton's burgeoning ability to craft narratives that transport readers to new worlds while echoing the familiar charm of their beloved city.

When not immersed in writing, Zayd Thornton is often found wandering the streets of Cape Town, drawing inspiration from its historic architecture, bustling markets, and panoramic views of the ocean.

A nod to OpenAI's ChatGPT for its invaluable assistance in the storytelling journey, ensuring every chapter sparkles with imagination

Read more at https://medium.com/@zaydthornton.